A PIRATE'S PRIZE

Pirates of Steel

Book 2

MARYSE DAWSON

Published by Blushing Books
An Imprint of
ABCD Graphics and Design, Inc.
A Virginia Corporation
977 Seminole Trail #233
Charlottesville, VA 22901

A Pirate's Prize
Pirates of Steel – Book Two
Maryse Dawson

eBook ISBN: 978-1-63954-461-5
Print ISBN: 978-1-63954-462-2

Prologue

THE WINTER NIGHT was falling and Sophia Thorn couldn't stop the shiver that took hold of her slender body but, still, she stood her ground, glaring at the pirate captain looming over her on the secluded beach.

With her feet bare, she could feel the cold sand clinging to her wet skin but her fiery temper kept her firmly rooted to the spot. She would not give in to his demands. As much as she loved him, she would not submit to Jack Steel's dominance.

He gave a low smile. "Continue like this and your spanking will be longer and harder, I assure you."

Sophia scowled and thrust out her bottom lip, ever defiant, but his words, as usual, sent a thrill of desire rushing through her, unbidden.

She ran her tongue over her lips and her eyes sparked fiercely back at him. "Fie, you cannot make me."

"Oh, I can." He stepped towards her and put his large hand on her upper arm, his tall form making her feel a little intimidated. "Come, my love. We must return to the ship."

She could tell by his tone, he was beginning to get impatient, but ever defiant, she tried to pull her arm away from him.

He tightened his grip so she kicked him. His reaction was to immediately lift her skirts and smack her bottom.

She gasped at the sudden pain and tried to shy away from him.

"Behave, Sophia," he warned her.

She tried to extricate herself from his grip by shoving him. This earned her another sharp smack. "Desist! Carry on in this manner and I am going to wallop your backside properly, right here, right now!"

"Oh, fie! Show yourself for the devil you are." She attempted to stomp on his boot but her bare feet made no impact except to make him angrier than he already was.

"Last warning!" he growled, pulling her towards the small boat on the shoreline.

Her strong-willed nature challenged his authority over her and almost of its own accord, her elbow went crashing into his side. His sharp intake of breath meant that she'd made an impact. Her triumphant smile, however, didn't last long.

Jack stopped walking and quickly upended her over one knee. She felt a rush of air as her skirts were thrown over her head and then a sharp sting when his hand descended in rapid succession on her bloomer-clad backside.

She hardly had time to draw a breath as he smacked her buttocks relentlessly. The noise reverberated across the sand and it was soon joined by her sharp cries. When Jack finally let her up, she was hopping from one foot to the other. Her face was crinkled up with pain and she was on the verge of tears.

"Now, move!" he ordered her.

Sophia thrust out her bottom lip but did as he said, walking over to the tender where Simmons, one of Jack's crew, was sucking vigorously on his clay pipe, doing his best to pretend he had seen and heard nothing.

Jack helped Sophia into the small boat and told Simmons to shove off. Jack stared at Sophia the whole way back to the ship, the only sound between them being Simmons' nervous, tuneless whistling.

Back in the captain's quarters, Jack eyed Sophia as she sat on the bed. She refused to make eye contact, instead focussing on a book cover on the far shelf.

"Can't you ever do as you're told?" he chided her.

Her eyes snapped to his and she pouted. "I only wanted to see where that path led. Why did you have to scold me?"

He walked over to her and drew her up into his arms. "Because you could have wandered off and got lost, which is something I couldn't bear." He trailed a finger down her cheek. "You are far too precious to me."

Every time he caressed her, chills raced up and down her spine. She would never tire of his touch but she would always rebel against his dominant nature. She was too feisty to submit to his every demand; after all, he wasn't always right. Besides, having a warm bottom aroused her passion for this handsome bear of a man.

She raised her hands and, placing them behind his neck, drew his head down for a kiss. Her lips fell open softly as he tenderly plundered them, kissing her soft mouth deeply and stirring in her a feeling of exquisite desire.

Lost in his embrace, her mind drifted back to when and how they had met…

Chapter 1

LA ROCHELLE, *France, 1823...*

The large frigate moved slowly from its dock, edging its way in the choppy waters to the narrow channel that led between the two lighthouses guarding the harbour.

The rain continued to beat down, the thunder booming overhead, the jagged streaks of lightning flashing across the sky.

Captain Jack Steel pulled his sou'wester more tightly around his shoulders, trying his best to keep the rain from dripping down the back of his neck, his tricorn doing very little to prevent it. It was highly uncomfortable but nothing he wasn't used to.

In the distance, he could see a thin, bright line on the horizon, the edge of the storm and his intended destination. It had been raining for two days solid and he could no longer afford to stay in port. Grimes had already warned him that there had been sightings of customs officers on the edge of town, so it was only a matter of time before they descended onto the quayside demanding to know what he had on board. A little thing like a storm wouldn't keep the bastards away and the last thing he needed was them swarming all over his ship. So, on the turn of the tide, he had weighed anchor and set sail.

He looked to his side as John, the quartermaster, joined him, holding his hat on tightly and shouting against the wind, "It's gonna be a tricky couple of hours, Cap'n."

"You can say that again!" Jack hollered back, his keen eye noting the swell of the ocean ahead, the white crested waves marking their allegiance to the stormy skies above.

The ship slipped past the two lighthouses unhindered and began its journey across the Atlantic Ocean—destination Williamsburg, Virginia.

Jack's crew worked like trojans, each playing his part in keeping the ship safe from the elements. Their very lives depended on their tenacity to do their job under such harsh conditions.

Sails were hoisted and secured as soon as the command was given, John's booming voice heard above the roar of the wind. A wind that whistled through the lines, whilst the wood creaked and protested as the menacing waves crashed against the hull.

Jack's senses were on full alert. Never, did he feel so alive as on days like this. The insistent flapping of the canvas and the roar of the waves set adrenaline coursing through his body, and when they came through the storm, it always heralded a feeling of achievement. A victory for all those on board.

Taking a deep breath, he held the wheel tight, and with grim determination, he kept their vessel on a straight path through the raging storm.

Thorn Creek Plantation, Williamsburg, Virginia…

Sophia Thorn thrummed her fingers on the exterior wooden balcony outside her bedroom and looked over at her father, watching his long strides make quick work of the path that led down to the tobacco fields.

Her eyes narrowed with loathing. He never failed to surprise her. He was an arrogant, overbearing man whom she had the displeasure to call her father. On the surface, he gave the impression that he was the perfect father but, beneath, lay a heart of stone. She and her twin brother, Isaac, could testify to that.

At twenty-three, Sophia and her brother had been motherless for ten years. Their mother, at least, had been able to protect them against his cruel nature—the buffer between good and bad. Her unexpected death at the tender age of thirty-three had left the young siblings bereft and at the mercy of their cruel father, Brian.

It had been a very long and arduous ten years since. Ten years in which the twins had grown up very quickly.

A movement to the left caught Sophia's eye and her face broke into a smile when she recognised her brother striding towards the house.

"Isaac!" she called out to him, waving enthusiastically, and was rewarded when he beamed back.

Quickly, she rushed into her bedroom and then down the spiral staircase to jump into his arms just as he strode through the main double doors.

"Whoa!" he cried, before lifting her up in the air and whirling her around. "Have I been away that long?"

"Yes!" she cried, "two whole weeks."

He grinned, his handsome face lighting up with happiness. "Did you miss me?"

She punched him on the arm. "Of course, I did." She pouted a little and added, "Although I wouldn't have had to miss you if you'd taken me with you!"

Isaac shook his head. "It's too dangerous, Sophia. Besides, you have enough to sort out, doing the paperwork and keeping his nib nose out of our business."

He put her down on the ground and, placing an arm around her shoulders, walked towards the opposite door. "I'm starving and I really need a cup of Loretta's coffee."

Loretta was their cook at Thorn Creek, and according to Isaac, she made the best coffee in all of Christendom. Sophia wouldn't know as she had never travelled anywhere else. But she did agree it was delicious.

They walked through the doorway and down the corridor until they reached the kitchens. Loretta was in the middle of preparing fresh bread, but on seeing Isaac, a broad grin broke out on her face, and quickly wiping her hands, she welcomed him with open arms. She made no bones about the fact she was pleased to see him. Loretta had been with the family for a long time, well before their mother had died. And she'd been the soft, assuring voice they had run to in times of distress. They both appreciated her and she knew it.

With his usual charm, Isaac asked her for some coffee and she immediately set to making a fresh brew for both of them, telling them to go into the parlour and that she would bring it in, with some special snacks for Isaac. She always spoiled him.

Sitting on the sofa in the parlour, Sophia waited whilst Isaac took a seat at the table before asking, "So, how did the trip go?"

"Very well indeed. *Sunfire* handled beautifully as usual. We've made a pretty penny this time."

Between them, they owned a ship called *Sunfire*. Something their father wasn't privy to. It was a dangerous life but fate had led them in this direction. Isaac had left home, shortly after their mother had died, to lead a life aboard the merchant vessel *Nonsuch*. He had learned everything from the bottom up and had earned himself a name for being a trust-worthy, hardworking, likeable member of the crew.

Several years later, under an insufferable new captain, a mutiny had taken place and the remaining crew had voted wholeheartedly for Isaac to take his place. One thing had led to another and the crew had decided to take ownership of the ship, changing her name from *Nonsuch* to *Sunfire* and turning to piracy to fund their lifestyle.

Isaac had continued to visit home as usual, and as far as his father was concerned, he was still working for the *Nonsuch*. It would remain that way until Isaac decided otherwise. His father was not to be trusted. Truth be told, he only visited the plantation to see his sister and to make sure she was safe. He couldn't abide his father.

As soon as they had enough money put aside, he planned to move her to her own house on another part of the bay. Sophia was quite shocked when he had revealed to her what had happened regarding the mutiny, but when she learned of his intentions to buy a house and make a new life for them both, away from their loathsome father, she was more than ready to become involved herself. She kept track of their money and helped find buyers for goods they had plundered. She was very adept at reading people and could tell if someone was trustworthy or not. Maybe that was to do with living with their father for so long, for she could spot a wrong'un a mile off.

At the moment, she was dependent upon their father for everything and it irked Isaac. Luckily, Sophia was highly spir-ited and she knew how to handle their father's temper. More often than not, simply by keeping her distance. He admired Sophia; she was not only beautiful but strong-willed. Without it, he feared she would have been browbeaten into a shadow of the beautiful woman she had become.

It was what spurred him on to keep plundering other

ships. That, and the fact he enjoyed every minute. He smiled and, remembering something, reached inside his long coat and brought out a small item wrapped in cloth. He handed it to her.

"I found this and thought you might like it."

Sophia's eyes lit up. "Oh, what is it?"

"Open it and see."

Sophia took the item and peeled off the cloth to reveal a jewelled hair pin. "Oh, it's beautiful!"

"Bodmin assures me the diamonds are real and not paste."

"I love it." She jumped up and walked over to a small oval mirror on the wall. Raising her hands, she neatly put the gold pin in her blonde hair. Her striking green eyes stared back at her. "It's so beautiful. Thank you, Isaac."

There came a knock on the door and Isaac called out, "Come!"

It was Loretta and she was carrying a tray with not only the sought after coffee, but several small pastries.

"There you are, Master Isaac. That'll keep you going until supper." She turned to him and queried, "You *are* having supper tonight?"

"Yes, I wouldn't miss one of your delicious meals," he laughed and then added, "but I won't be staying. My ship leaves tonight."

When she'd left, Sophia raised her eyes to his. "Where are you anchored?"

"Usual place, *Archer's Hope*."

"Is there any cargo to unload, or did you sell everything?"

"Sold it all to our usual contacts. I will return later tonight with the trunk. Store it in the usual place and bank it weekly into my account so as not to arouse suspicion."

They heard footsteps in the hallway and both quickly went silent. The door opened and their father appeared. He swept his cold gaze over Isaac and remarked, "Thought you would humble yourself and pay us a visit, did you?"

Sophia regarded him, her expression veiled. He was so rude. Always had been and always would be. She wondered for the umpteenth time what sort of life her mother must have led and pitied her. They had witnessed a lot, but she knew her mother had kept more hidden from them.

Isaac sipped on his coffee, and his voice, equally as cold, said, "I never humble myself, Father. I have returned home to see how my sister fares." Before her father could respond, Isaac asked, "Coffee?"

Their eyes met and her father thought better of retaliating. "Black, no sugar."

Taking the coffee, her father took a seat opposite her and leaned back in the chair. "How's life on board the *Nonsuch*?"

"Very well. We are sailing to Jamaica tonight. With the cross winds, it shouldn't take too long."

"What business is she doing there?"

"Usual. Whatever the captain decides to buy and trade in. I'm not privy to the details, I'm just there to do my job." Isaac shot a look at Sophia and winked. She hid a smile and looked down at her hands resting in her lap. Not long now, and she would be away from this place and free to do as she pleased. She couldn't wait.

That night, Isaac returned as promised with a small trunk full of silver coins. Their father was already asleep so, quietly, Sophia led Isaac around the back of the house and into one of the big barns. Easing an insignificant stone out of the wall, Isaac lifted the trunk into the cavity and then replaced the stone. It was the perfect hiding place. No trace could be seen of their stash whatsoever.

Sitting down on the dusty barn floor, Isaac withdrew a bottle of rum from inside his coat and settling herself beside him, Sophia produced two goblets. It was a ritual with them and an enjoyable one at that.

Pouring them a healthy draught each, Isaac grinned and said, "To us and the future."

Sipping the fiery liquid slowly, Sophia leaned her head against the barn wall and sighed softly. "How much longer do you think it will take to make enough money to leave this godforsaken hole?"

"I don't know, maybe one more year. We nearly have enough, don't we?"

Sophia nodded. "Nearly." She angled her head to look at him. "Can you not move a little faster? Plunder a few more ships?"

Isaac slapped his thigh and laughed aloud. "You make it sound so easy! You have no idea what is involved or how dangerous it is, Sophia."

"Then take me with you on a journey! Just one. Please? You know I want to explore. I've never even set foot off this land. I simply sit here and wait for you to regale me with tales of your exploits and daring. It's unfair," she huffed.

"I have enough to worry about without the addition of trying to keep you safe whilst on board."

"I can look after myself!" she responded heatedly. "You know I can wield a sword as well as any man. You've taught me well over the years."

"Sophia, you are tiny. Yes, you can parry a sword very well, but against the strength of a burly pirate, how long do you think you could last?" He shook his head. "Just bear with me for another few months, even a year if it has to be, but we will break free from our father. I promise you."

Sophia took another draught of rum and closed her eyes.

Could she stand it? She had stood twenty-three years of it so she supposed another few months wouldn't matter.

"Very well, if I must. The nearer my escape gets, the more restless I become. Not long now." She raised her goblet to his. "To us, dear brother, and solitude!"

"Amen to that."

The next day dawned bright and sunny. Sophia waited quietly until her father had left to oversee their plantation, and saddling her small mare, *Bounty*, she rode into Jamestown. Her stash of silver coins was safely stored in her saddlebag. They never deposited it all in one go as she didn't want to raise any suspicion as to where the source of the money came from. Doing it in smaller amounts here and there, never raised an eyebrow from the bank teller. And that was exactly how they wanted it to be. It was a separate bank from her father's, but even so, one could never be too careful.

She always enjoyed the ride to town. The plantation was on the outskirts of Williamsburg and so it was only a short journey to Jamestown. She liked nothing better than to walk along the wharf admiring the many ships that were moored in the bay. Some were absolutely massive and quite awe inspiring. She found it fascinating watching the crew climbing up the rigging when the ships set sail, or simply perusing the people who sat in the small boats navigating their way between the much larger vessels.

She pulled a face. If only Isaac would let her go on a trip with him. It need only be a short one. Just to see the Caribbean islands, would be a treat. It was all right for him to deny her, but he wasn't the one having to bear the brunt of their father when he was in one of his moods, which seemed to be more and more often lately. It was truly wearing. He was never nice to any of the plantation workers. They weren't paid much and he took advantage of them wherever and whenever he could. Her eyes narrowed. No, her father wasn't a nice man at all.

She took a deep breath and tried to erase him from her mind for a moment, gazing at the surrounding scenery and breathing in the heady scent of the wildflowers scattered amongst the picturesque marshland.

Reaching town, she dismounted, and tethering her horse, she went inside the bank. Ten minutes later, and her deposit was done. No questions asked. Satisfied, she walked down the steps onto the street and just as she was about to reach for Bounty's reins, someone shouted behind her. She whirled around just in time to see a runaway horse heading straight for her. Before she had time to react, a hand grabbed her around the waist and whisked her out of harm's way.

She fell backwards in the process but strong arms kept her from falling to the ground.

Gasping with shock, she looked up to find herself in the embrace of one of the handsomest men she had ever laid eyes upon.

For a moment, they stared at each other, not saying a word. He looked almost as startled as she did. Sophia felt a blush suffuse her already hot cheeks and quickly tried to right herself. Lord, he was handsome.

He helped her to her feet and regarded her with gorgeous brown eyes flecked with hazel. "Are you unharmed?" he asked. "I saw the horse coming and I acted instinctively. I hope I didn't hurt you in the process."

Sophia swallowed hard. "No, not at all. I must thank you for saving me." She looked over her shoulder to see the horse in the distance. There was a trail of dust in its wake where its hooves had churned up the ground. "Goodness, I wonder who it belongs to."

"I have no idea, but they'll have a hard time catching it by the looks of things."

Sophia turned back to him. He was so tall that she had to angle her neck to look at him. Her eyes roamed over his face, noting his strong jaw and brown, sun-kissed hair tied back with a leather strap.

His eyes crinkled at the corners and he smiled, showing even, white teeth. "Allow me to introduce myself. Jack Steel."

Sophia's pulse seemed to be racing and she tried to calm herself. How could she have such a reaction to a man she had only just met. She really had to compose herself. She smiled back and shyly replied, "I am Sophia Thorn."

"Thorn? You're not from Thorn Creek Plantation by any chance?"

Sophia nodded.

"Well, I never. So you're Brian Thorn's daughter?" He tilted his head, studying her.

"Yes, I am. Do you know him?"

"Yes, fairly well. We have business dealings on occasion. In fact, I'm going there this afternoon." He regarded her silently. "I knew he had a son and daughter, but I never would have believed his daughter would be quite so beautiful."

"Oh." Sophia blushed hotly under his perusal, and unused to such compliments, she didn't quite know how to answer.

Jack looked down at Sophia Thorn and couldn't quite believe that such a beautiful creature could come from such an odious man as Brian. Her green eyes, edged with long, dark lashes, were exquisite and matched her dark green riding habit perfectly. Her small, heart-shaped face, golden blonde hair and perfectly plump, soft lips had made his heart stop for one moment.

It was strange because he couldn't recall ever having experienced such a sudden surge of emotions. It felt as though someone had come up and slapped him around the face. He'd met pretty women before but Sophia was beyond compare.

She seemed to possess a sweet nature, unlike her father, who was one of the meanest men he'd ever had the misfortune to come across. A right nasty bastard on all accounts. But he bought Jack's booty and never asked any questions. He usually drove a hard bargain, which always came out in Brian's favour, of course. But that was the nature of his business and it proved that there were more thieves on land than at sea in one way or another.

Jack looked down at the demure woman in front of him, and always one to make the most of an opportune moment, especially when a pretty woman was involved, he asked her if she would like to have lunch with him.

Her face looked a little shocked. "Oh, um… I—"

He interrupted her, "I know we've only just met, but I'm already acquainted with your father, and after lunch, I can escort you back home. After all, I'm going there anyway."

He watched her face, noting the little frown on her forehead, the way her eyes darted nervously to her hands whilst she tried to come to a decision. Raising her eyes to his, she finally agreed to come. He could see it was a decision she hadn't come to lightly and it heartened him, for it would seem she, too, felt their connection.

Fate had literally thrown her in his path and he wasn't going to ignore such a momentous opportunity.

Holding his arm out and smiling broadly, he waited for her to place her hand on his sleeve, but the moment never happened.

For, suddenly, a deep voice boomed, "So this is where you are!"

Both of them looked up to find her father glaring down at them from his high vantage point upon his horse. The atmosphere quickly changed and Jack was immediately wary. Brian oozed anger and it seemed to be directed at Sophia.

"You're coming back home now," he ordered her.

"But, Father, I—" Sophia began, flustered.

Her father immediately interrupted her. "Do as I tell you or you'll take the consequences." His eyes were blazing. Something had clearly upset him and Jack had no idea what. He tried to intervene.

"Mr. Thorn, we were just going to have lunch together. Perhaps you would like to join us?"

Brian turned his cold gaze on Jack, and with most men, it would have made them tremble with fear, but not so with Jack. Steel by name, steel by nature. He was used to tackling men such as Brian and kept his gaze unwavering.

"Neither of us will be joining you for lunch, Mr. Steel, and if you wish to do our usual transaction this afternoon then I suggest you hold your tongue."

Jack's eyes narrowed and he was about to respond when Sophia placed her hand in his and gave it a small squeeze. His eyes met hers and he understood her silent message to remain quiet. Perhaps he would make things worse if he retaliated.

Sophia, clearly embarrassed, quickly walked over to her horse and untethered it. Mounting quickly, she urged her horse towards her father's. As they rode away, she turned to look back at Jack, a wistful expression on her face.

Jack stared after them until they were but a dot in the distance. How rude for a father to treat his daughter so in public. Whatever had she done to cause him to act like that?

But then this was Brian Thorn. He was a ruthless, hard bastard.

Even though he had only just met Sophia, Jack already felt protective of her and he knew that he wouldn't be satisfied until he'd assured himself of her well-being. So one thing was certain, he wasn't going to leave Thorn Creek Plantation without first making sure that the pretty little Sophia was unharmed.

Chapter 2

SOPHIA COULDN'T REMEMBER the last time she had felt so embarrassed. She closed her eyes for a moment, holding the reins tightly, and then her jaw set tight, she glared across at her father. In that moment, she felt she hated him more than she had ever done in her entire life.

Jack Steel would never want to go anywhere with her now, let alone a restaurant. Why would a man get involved with a woman when her father was so odious?

"Why do you want me to come home so urgently?" she asked at last, her temper now overcoming her embarrassment.

He angled his head to look at her, his eyes narrowed. "Because I have found out, my devious daughter, what you've been up to!" He emitted a low laugh. "I find it amusing that you thought you could keep it hidden from me."

Sophia's breath caught in her throat, and trying her best to put on an outward appearance of calm, she asked, "What do you mean?"

"Stealing from me. I had my suspicions but I decided to follow you this morning. I wanted to see for myself."

"I've never stolen anything from you! What are you talking about?"

He held his hand up. "We'll discuss this when we get home. I have no desire to talk further with you so I suggest you keep quiet. You're in enough trouble already."

Sophia thought about arguing further, but it wouldn't bode well for later. So, as hard as it was, she remained silent until they reached the plantation. Her mind was working overtime trying to think why he would think she had stolen from him. He must have seen her go into the bank but she could explain that away easily. No, there must be something else.

Reaching the drive in front of the house, they both dismounted and gave the reins to a waiting servant. Her father grabbed her upper arm and led her towards the side of the house. Sophia's stomach lurched when he hustled her towards the barn. The barn where she and Isaac kept the trunk. For a moment, she tried to dig her heels in, but he just glared at her and propelled her roughly forward.

Dear God. Had he discovered their hidden stash? How was she going to explain so much money?

Her father propelled her into the barn and marched her over to the exact spot where the trunk was hidden. Sophia was now in no doubt.

Letting her go, he reached down and, with a bit of effort, pulled out the stone to reveal the trunk. He set it on the ground and opened the lid. It was empty. Sophia's jaw dropped open. "Where's the money?"

Brian's eyes sparked with malice. "It has been returned to the rightful owner—me."

"But that's not your money, it's mine!"

He gave her a hard, cold stare. "What money could you possibly have?"

Sophia stared back at him helplessly. What could she say?

She certainly didn't want to implicate Isaac. Their whole plan would fall apart. Now her goal was so close, nothing was going to get in her way.

"I-I have been saving up. I—"

"I don't give you an allowance, so what exactly have you been saving?"

She frantically searched for an explanation, but could come up with nothing that sounded even remotely feasible. She tried anyway. "Isaac has been giving me a small allowance."

Her father clapped his hands together and let out a loud laugh. "Bravo, Sophia. You think I'm that gullible to believe that my son, who scrapes a living on board a merchant ship, would have enough money left to give to you? And not only that, but a whole trunk of silver coins?" He shook his head and pointed a finger in her face, his eyes turning nasty. "You've been caught red-handed, you ungrateful little madam." He folded his arms across his chest. "I should have you whipped for this!"

Sophia paled and laid a hand on her chest with fear, her vivid green eyes staring at him like he was the devil incarnate. "I swear to you, I have not stolen from you! How could I?"

"You know where I keep the safe. I don't know how you got the key, but somehow you must have. It's the only explanation for that amount of silver."

Sophia stomped her foot and balled her hands into fists by her side. "You're wrong! You cannot accuse me of such a thing."

"Oh, but I do. The evidence is clear to see, and like I say, I should have you whipped." He glared at her, seemingly enjoying her discomfort. "Luckily for you, I have another solution. I'm going to send you to the Johnson reform school in Richmond for six months. They can teach you some manners and how 'thou shalt not steal'."

"W-what?" Her mind was in a state of shock.

"You heard me. The carriage will take you tomorrow afternoon, so I suggest you start packing." He didn't wait to hear her response. He had made his decision and whatever she had to say was of no consequence.

Sophia heard him leave but she stood frozen to the spot. A reform school? She had heard rumours of them and they were never good. But to think he would stoop as low as to send his only daughter to such a place, was unthinkable.

She had to get word to Isaac, but his ship set sail last night. He wouldn't return home for at least another week or two, by which time she would be long gone.

She stood there, her mind working fast. How could she get out of going? Run away? But where to?

She placed her head in her hands and tried to stop the tears slipping down her cheeks but it was impossible. As brave as she tried to be, this time, fate wasn't on her side. She collapsed to her knees and gave in to the tears.

Five minutes later and feeling somewhat calmer and more clear-headed, she angrily brushed the tears away. She was made of sterner stuff than this. Isaac always told her so. Now was the time to stand up for herself.

Thinking hard, she knew that the only way she could escape her father's orders was to run away. She also knew that if she were to succeed then it would have to be by ship. She wouldn't be able to get far enough away on her horse. Her father had too many associates in the area and a lot of those were in his pocket, so to speak. Somehow, they would find out and she would get caught. She just knew it.

She bit her bottom lip. But how to get on board a ship without anyone knowing? A disguise? Her eyes lit up. Of course. She was slender and petite. She could smuggle herself on board dressed like a boy. What would she say if she was caught trying to board? The best strategy was to act with confidence. She could say the quartermaster or captain had said she could come aboard. It all depended who was there to witness her arrival. She sighed and rolled her eyes heavenwards. Did she have the guts to pull it off? Did she have the confidence? Did she have a bloody choice?

She kicked some dust up in the air with frustration. Why did she have to have such an odious father?

Well, one thing was certain. Under no circumstances, was she going just to sit back and let him dictate her future. She had had enough now and this was the final straw.

With a determined look on her face, she set off back towards the house and went in search of some of Isaac's clothes. Alterations would be needed, but she was quite good with a needle and thread, so time was of the essence.

Jack arrived late afternoon at the Thorn premises, accompanied by several of his men with carts full of merchandise. Merchandise that he hoped to make a good sum out of—all depending on what Brian Thorn would offer him, of course. After this morning's altercation, he expected it would be even less than usual.

Sophia ran to her bedroom window when she heard the commotion on the drive, her needle and thread still in her hands. She had nearly completed one outfit but wanted to have two. She had no idea how long she would be in disguise or even where she was going to end up. But she would worry about that later. She didn't have the luxury of time to think about it.

She spotted Jack as he dismounted, her heart immediately racing at the sight of him. He was so handsome and cut such a fine figure. For a moment, she was wistful, imagining a life with someone so gallant and thoughtful. But reality suddenly hit and she closed her eyes, emitting a long, drawn out sigh. This wasn't the time to dwell on fairy tales, this was time to make haste and get away from her father's evil clutches.

Returning to the desk in her bedroom, she began to sew the next garment, her eyes focussed on the task at hand. She only had a few hours left to get everything ready, for she intended to leave at midnight, by foot, towards Archer's Hope. There were usually a few ships anchored not far from shore. The water was deep, easily accommodating the big vessels, and normally, there were a few small rowing boats tied up on the shoreline. She just hoped there would be one there tonight. She could swim but the idea of arriving on board looking like a drowned rat wasn't going to help her plan. Especially as wet clothing would stick to her body and reveal her feminine curves. Her eyes widened at the thought.

Half an hour later, she had finished altering her brother's clothes and packed one set in the bottom of a carpet bag, along with two dresses, undergarments, a nightgown, shoes, stockings, hairbrush, tooth stick and a short jacket. She would wear strong boots on her journey and her brother's long coat for warmth. To conceal her hair, she would tie it up and then wrap a scarf around her head. And to conceal her bosom, she would have to also tie a scarf around her chest.

For a moment, fear consumed her and she clapped a hand to her mouth to contain a sudden bout of nausea. Sitting down on a chair, she closed her eyes, feeling very despondent. Who was she kidding? How was she going to pull this off? What if she ended up in a worse predicament than going to the reform school?

At that thought, her eyes sprang open and her rebellious spirit came to the fore. Fie. Her father wasn't going to control her like this. If she ended up worse off, then so be it. In all truth, she didn't give a damn. She just wanted out.

Suddenly, she heard his voice calling up the stairs, "Sophia? *Sophia?*"

Quickly, she hurled her carpet bag under the bed and walked over to the door just as he opened it.

"Mr. Steel wishes to see you before he leaves." He smiled, but it didn't reach his eyes. "He wishes to ascertain that you are in good health after the encounter today."

"Oh, I see."

"I have refrained from revealing that you are a thief but please, be my guest, if you wish to tell him. It's your reputation that will be sullied, not mine."

Sophia's lip began to curl with disgust but she somehow managed to quell it. Once again, he was showing his true nature and it only confirmed to her that her plan to leave that night was the best course of action she could take. Another day in his company, was one too many.

Closing the bedroom door behind herself, she descended the staircase, her father right behind her. Jack Steel was outside on the front steps and he turned to face her when she approached, his eyes searching hers for any sign of maltreatment.

Sophia put on a brave smile and greeted him shyly. "Good evening, Mr. Steel."

"Miss Thorn."

Her father stood right next to them, looking from one to the other, his eyes narrowing. "As you can see, Mr. Steel, my daughter is in the best of health. If I had beaten her, you would know about it."

For a moment, a look of sheer hatred entered Sophia's eyes but she quickly hid it and responded, "It was just a misunderstanding earlier, Mr. Steel. My father and I have since spoken and everything is as it should be." She looked down at her hands. "I'm truly sorry you were witness to such a spectacle."

Jack's gaze never wavered as she spoke. "You have nothing to apologise for," he said, his voice soft but firm. "I just wanted to see for myself that you were unharmed."

He turned his gaze on her father and his expression turned hard. "If you ever lay a hand upon your daughter and I find out about it, be warned that I *will* seek retribution. Have no doubt."

Sophia swallowed hard. She had never heard anyone speak like that to her father and she wondered how he was going to react. Her eyes wide, she watched his face turn a deep shade of red with rage and he glared at Jack with unconcealed anger. "How dare you tell me how to bring up my daughter! Consider this the last transaction we ever do. Take your ill-gotten gains elsewhere next time—you'll never get such a good deal from anyone else!"

"I care not. You're a despicable excuse for a human being." Jack turned to Sophia and said, "I bid you good day, Miss Thorn." And with one last hard look at her father, he turned on his heel and headed for his horse and the men waiting for him.

Sophia watched him leave and wondered if she would ever meet such a great man again. Would their paths ever cross? She gave a small sigh. She doubted it. She didn't even know what town he came from.

No, her fate had something else entirely in store for her and it was going to begin tonight.

Ignoring her father completely, she headed back into the house to finish her packing. All she had left to do before she departed was raid the kitchen for a few provisions to tide her over the next few days. Just in case her plan went awry.

Her meeting with Jack Steel tonight had made her even more determined to leave.

Archer's Hope...

It was well past midnight by the time Sophia reached the shore at Archer's Hope. In full disguise and with her bag flung over her shoulder, she looked every bit the young lad that she wished to portray. She was relieved to see there were three little rowing boats tied up which would enable her to get to one of the big frigates anchored a little off shore.

In the moonlight, she wondered which one to choose to stow away on. There were about three of them that she deemed suitable. One was very much like Isaac's ship, *Sunfire*. It had sleek lines and was nearly the same size, albeit slightly bigger. She placed her bag on the sand and settled herself next to it, avidly watching to see how quiet each ship was. If there were too many crew on deck, then she would have no chance of scrambling onboard without being noticed.

The ships' lanterns reflected on the water's surface and illuminated parts of the deck. Along with the moonlight, it was enough to see what was happening on each vessel.

The ship that had caught her eye seemed the most quiet, and so far, she had noticed only two men who seemed to be on watch. It was definitely the most suitable for her plan. She couldn't make out the ship's name as it was in shadow, but she could clearly see the merchant flag.

Taking a deep breath, she stood up and, picking up her bag, walked over to one of the little boats.

Sophia arrived at the ship's hull twenty minutes later, out of breath and very nervous. So much so that her lips were quivering, her hands trembling. The ship looked enormous up close, and for a moment, as she glanced up at its huge form, she almost decided to turn tail and row back to the shore, but she was made of sterner stuff than that. She had come this far, nothing was going to stop her now.

So far, no one had spotted her or certainly hadn't called out the alarm. Pulling the oars in and laying them on the bottom of the boat, she reached out to grab the rope ladder with one hand and grabbed for her bag with the other. It was a tricky maneuver but she somehow managed it without overbalancing. As she stepped onto the ladder, she kicked the rowboat away with all her might to send it away from the ship, so as not to alert the crew of her arrival. Nimbly, she climbed the ladder, her bag over her back, and reaching the top, she tentatively peered over the railings.

So far, so good. Silently, she jumped over the railing and landed on the deck, crouching low to avoid detection by the watchmen. Glancing around nervously, she decided which route to take. There was a raised platform on one side and she could just make out the silhouette of a man. So she quickly decided to go to the other side. Darting towards a wooden mast, she hunkered down next to it and peered across the deck. In the dim light, she could just make out a stairwell. If she could get down there, she could maybe find a cabin or storage room to hide out in. Her heart in her mouth, she stepped out, and then, seemingly out of nowhere, she felt a hand descend on the back of her jacket. She was lifted off the ground and spun around.

"And just where might ye be goin'?" a man asked with a deep growl. He was huge.

Sophia gasped and tried to wriggle free, but he wasn't having any of it. "Let me go! Let me go!" she cried.

Another man approached, grinning. "What ye got there, Grimes? Caught yerself a rare kind of fish, 'ave ye?"

"Reckon so, Callum. Whadya reckon I should do wi' it?"

"Throw it back. Do ye wanna 'and?"

Sophia was scared near to death and tried to wriggle free once more, but the man called Grimes had her well and truly captured. He grinned at her and moved to the railings, half shoving her over the side.

"Long way down, ain't it?" He laughed.

"Ah quit scarin' 'im," said another voice. "'E's only young, let 'im be."

"Trust old Smithy to 'ave a soft spot," Callum remarked.

Sophia found herself suddenly pulled back and her feet planted on the firm wooden deck. Her breathing was erratic and her eyes wide in her face. Surrounded by the three large men, she didn't know what to say so just stood there mutely staring back at them. One thing she did know for certain, though, was that she was scared out of her wits.

Grimes placed a hand on her shoulder. "We're only playin' wi' ye, lad. We wouldn't throw ye overboard."

"What ye doin' 'ere anyway?" Smithy asked. "Runnin' away from someone, are ye?"

Sophia nodded, not daring to speak. The man had an eye patch, making him look more sinister than he actually was, because his voice sounded quite kind.

Grimes patted her shoulder. "We've 'ad a few like ye on board over the years. Reckon another one won't matter." He propelled her towards Smithy. "Take 'im down below and give 'im somat to eat."

Sophia was relieved to see that her disguise was working. No one had noticed anything amiss. She just hoped it would be the same in the daylight, for at the moment, the night was her blessed companion.

Her legs felt like jelly as Smithy led her towards the stairs, and behind her, she heard Grimes order Callum back to watch duty. "Captain Jack ain't got time for slackers, Callum. Look lively, lad, look lively!" His voice was gruff but she detected an element of camaraderie.

Following Smithy down the steps, she faltered for a moment as a thought entered her mind. Grimes had said *Captain Jack. Jack?* What if the captain was Jack Steel? Her heart almost stopped. No! That would be too much of a coincidence. After all, there were many men called Jack... surely?

But Jack had sold goods to her father... and this was a merchant vessel. She had seen the flag with her own eyes.

Oh, lord!

If indeed it was Jack Steel and he discovered her on board his ship, he might just see through her disguise and send her back to her father. Or would he? She had borne witness to the fact that he hated him as much as she did. But would he want her on board his ship?

Please God, she hoped it wasn't him. For if it was, then she could be in even more trouble than she thought. She pictured her father's face. Retribution would be tenfold compared to her initial punishment.

Trying to shake off the feeling of unease, she decided that she was just overreacting because of the situation she had put herself in, and squaring her shoulders, she followed Smithy down into the bowels of the hulking great ship that she intended to use as a temporary home.

Jack sat at the desk in his cabin and looked at the maps laid out in front of him. His course was plotted for Portsmouth. They would stop off in France to fill up with provisions, and along their route, he would find a ship or two to plunder. The thought made him smile with anticipation.

His mind turned to Sophia Thorn. They had only met briefly, but she had made a big impact on him. Her vibrant green eyes were not something he would forget in a long while. Her father was such an odious man. Life wasn't fair. How could she be the product of his loins?

A knock sounded on the door and he called out, "Come!"

It was John, the quartermaster. "Are you ready to depart, Cap'n?"

"Yes, John. Hustle the crew up and let's get going." He stood up and rubbed his hands together. "I need a change of scenery. This place has left a bad taste in my mouth."

"Aye, aye, Cap'n."

Picking up his tricorn hat off the desk, he placed it on his head and, with a broad grin, followed John out of the cabin. With something else to focus on, he could push all thoughts of the green-eyed beauty out of his mind... for now.

Chapter 3

SOPHIA NERVOUSLY FOLLOWED Smithy down several steps and along a narrow corridor until they reached the galley. The chef gave her a cursory glance and then returned to pounding some dough, putting so much energy into the task that Sophia thought he might make a hole in the table.

Smithy picked up a mug and filled it with something from a tall bottle before handing it to her and telling her to take a seat. She quickly did as she was told, sliding onto a long bench and nestling herself as inconspicuously as possible into the corner, tucking her carpet bag by her feet. Picking up the mug, she sniffed the contents. It smelled like rum. Tentatively, she tipped the cup and took a mouthful. Yes, it was definitely rum and a strong one at that. As the fiery liquid slipped down her throat, even though her eyes watered a little from the strength, it did a great deal to calm her nerves.

Smithy placed a pewter plate in front of her with some cheese, bread and an apple. He grinned at her. "Now get that down yer neck and don't wander off. I'll be back in a jiffy."

That had been about an hour or so ago, during which time, from her shadowy retreat, Sophia had watched men pass to and fro through the galley and it wasn't long before she had felt the movement of the ship. They had set sail.

Sophia's nerves were still jittery despite the large helping of rum, but she was so glad she had run away. The very notion of being confined to a reform school for six months was horrendous and it showed her father for the tyrant he was. So, as scary as her current situation was, she would still choose it over that any day.

Sophia listened to the ship's hull creaking as it made its way along the James River towards the open sea, the overhead lanterns swinging and casting their light around the dim interior. What would life out on the vast ocean feel like? For the first time in her life, she would find out. All she had to do now was keep her head down and act like the poor lad she was trying to portray, then disembark at the first port where they docked. Most probably easier said than done, but desperate times called for desperate measures.

Smithy finally returned to the galley and settled himself down opposite her. "So, what's ye name then, lad?"

"Isaac, sir. Isaac Jeffries." Sophia looked at him with big eyes, hoping her voice sounded boyish. It seemed to work.

"Well, Isaac, who are ye runnin' from?"

"My father. He threatened to beat me and I-I ran away."

"How old are ye?"

"Thirteen, sir."

He angled his head and gave her a quizzical look. "Yer quite small for thirteen. Bet ye father ain't fed ye enough. Am I right?"

Sophia nodded. "He's a right bastard, sir."

Smithy raised a surprised eyebrow and then broke out in laughter. "Sounds like ye escaped just in the nick of time, lad.

No one likes being around a bastard, let me tell ye." He rubbed his forehead and then said, "Well, ye can bunk in wi' me. There's a spare bed. If anyone wants somat doin', yer to do it, do ye understand. Be it emptying the piss pots or fetching some vittles, de ye follow, lad? Ye've got to earn yer keep 'round 'ere."

Sophia nodded, even though, inside, she was recoiling from even the notion of emptying a piss pot. Good lord.

"And keep out o' the way of the crew. When we attack, ye don't wanna be anywhere near the deck—ye could easily lose an eye. Look at me." He pointed to his eye patch. "Lost it when a shard of wood was blown into it. I was lucky to be alive according to Philippe, two centimetres deeper and I'd be a gonna."

"W-what do you mean, when you attack?" Sophia asked.

He gave a deep belly laugh. "Yer aboard a pirate ship now, lad. Didn't ye realise?"

Sophia swallowed hard. "I thought it was a merchant vessel."

"Well, it is, of sorts. We take someone else's goods n' sell 'em." He studied her, still grinning and seemingly finding her innocence rather amusing. "Don't worry, lad. Like I say, keep outta the crew's way unless asked and yer'll be fine." He stood up. "Now, follow me and I'll show ye yer quarters."

In a daze, Sophia picked up her bag and followed after him, trying to keep up with his long strides. She soon found herself in a small cabin with two bunks and barely enough room to move.

"Top bunk's yours. Get yerself some sleep. If ye need a piss, the pot's over there in the corner." And on that note, he turned on his heel and left, closing the door after him. For a moment, Sophia just stared at the door, not moving, her mind still reeling from the fact she was on a pirate ship.

What was she going to do now? How long was it going to be before they intended to dock? If their intention was to plunder other ships, then it could be weeks before she stepped foot on dry land. She placed a hand over her mouth. What had she got herself into?

Jack awoke from a restful sleep and stretched, before rolling onto his side and staring out of the lattice windows. The weather was sunny, the sky a clear, vivid shade of blue, and he could feel the steady motion as *Blythe Spirit* slipped through the waves with ease, meaning they had a good breeze on their side.

Sliding his legs from the bed, he strode over to the door and, opening it, hollered up the steps, "Smithy! Bring me some hot water if you please."

It was their usual ritual. Smithy was usually in the vicinity, ready to serve him. If he wasn't, one of the others would bellow the command along the line until it reached him.

A little while later, Smithy appeared with a jug and bowl. Placing them on the desk, he quickly left to collect Jack's breakfast which the chef was already preparing.

Jack completed his morning ablutions and began to dress, stepping into his black britches. He was tucking in his shirt when Smithy returned, only, this time, he had a young lad with him.

Jack gave the boy a cursory glance. Smithy nearly always had a young helper. With a crew of a hundred men, there were usually a few youngsters on board. Either relatives or just young boys with a yearning to discover life at sea. So, it was nothing unusual.

Concentrating on fastening his waistcoat, he listened as

Smithy admonished the young lad. Jack smiled to himself.
Smithy could be a right taskmaster when he wanted to be.
But it was the way of the ship and that was how the young
boys learned, from the bottom up, everything there was to
know about running a ship and the ranking system.

"Put that down there and don't drop it!" Smithy snapped.

"Yes, sir," the lad said.

Jack looked up just in time to see the boy follow Smithy
out of his quarters. He was small and quite slender. Reckon
he needed feeding up a bit. He shook his head. There was a
lot of poverty about, and being on board a ship, at least they
could be sure of a ready meal or two. The work might be
hard, but they could learn a trade.

Taking a seat at his desk, he poured himself a coffee and
began to break his fast.

Sophia's heart was racing and she could feel her cheeks were
hot. She couldn't believe it when Smithy had told her they
would be serving the captain's breakfast. At first, she had
thought of trying to wriggle out of it but then decided it
might make Smithy suspicious of her, and also, she was
curious to know just who the captain was.

Now she knew.

How the devil had she managed to get on a ship where
the captain was Jack Steel? Had fate lent a hand? Was it a
good thing or a bad thing?

If he found out that she was on board his ship, would he
be more likely to send her back home or not? Oh, good lord.
Her stomach was roiling nervously.

Luckily for her, Jack hadn't paid her much attention, and
as soon as she'd realised he was the captain, she'd kept her
head down and her eyes lowered. She nibbled on a fingernail

and thought about Jack's transactions with her father. Did her father know he was a pirate?

Her mind wandered to their last conversation at the plantation, her eyes widening when she remembered her father's words to Jack about taking his ill-gotten gains elsewhere. Oh, yes, her father knew all right.

Jack didn't act how she thought a pirate would. He seemed very gallant in fact. She frowned. Something didn't seem right.

"Ye've got a lot on yer mind, lad. What're ye worried about?" Smithy asked her, as they returned to the galley. "Yer not feeling sea sick, are ye?"

"No, no. I'm hungry, that's all."

Smithy laughed and pointed at the bench table. "Sit yerself down then and I'll fetch us somat to eat."

Sophia slid along the bench and thought about her situation. So far, her disguise was working. Sleeping in the small cabin last night had been highly uncomfortable, not so much the little bed, but being in the same cabin with a strange man. She had slept in her clothes and even though she'd managed to run a cloth over her face from a mug of water, she still felt grimy. But if this was how it was going to have to be, then she just had to deal with it and think only of her goal—to start a new life with her brother.

Smithy returned and placed a plate of scrambled eggs in front of her along with a fresh bread roll. "Enjoy it while it lasts, lad. Once this runs out, we'll be on the gruel!"

Sophia pulled a face but quickly dug into the food. Although it had been a cover up for her thoughts, she had spoken the truth when she told Smithy she was starving and she had soon polished off the whole lot. When they'd finished, Sophia was given her first job, washing up. Smithy left her in the hands of the cook who gruffly said his name was Seamus and he showed her a big mound of plates and mugs.

"Look lively, lad, we ain't got all day!"

Sophia quickly picked up the cloth and began to clean the plates in the bucket of hot soapy water, without daring to complain. Whatever they told her to do, she was going to have to get used to doing it. Her nose wrinkled at the thought of the piss pots, but swallowing back a bit of bile, she focussed on the task at hand.

"When ye've done that, ye can go up on deck and get me some more eggs," Seamus said.

"Eggs? From where?"

"From the chickens, of course. Yer wet behind the ears, ain't ye, lad?" Seamus laughed. "The chicken coops are in the middle of the foredeck. Ye can't miss 'em. Don't let any of the bleeders out when yer doing it, either."

Sophia's eyes widened. She didn't really want to go out on deck. If Jack was there, it wouldn't be so easy to avoid him. Down here in the dim interior, even if he did venture down, she could easily slide into a shady corner or hide behind a crate or large sack. Up on deck, it wasn't going to be so easy.

Finishing her chore, she wiped her hands on a dry cloth and went to leave. Seamus stopped her. "Ain't ye forgettin' somat?"

She turned and looked, to find him holding out a small wooden box.

"Oh! I see. For the eggs," she exclaimed.

Seamus shook his head and shot her a look of exasperation. "Aye, for the eggs."

Sophia heard him muttering under his breath as she left, but she paid him no heed. She was new to this, so he'd just have to learn some patience.

Jack stood on the quarterdeck, his arms folded over his broad chest, his legs astride for balance, and looked out to the horizon. *Blythe Spirit* was cutting through the waves at a quick rate, making good time.

Taking his spyglass from his pocket, he lifted it to his right eye and scanned the ocean. It was empty. Nothing worth plundering yet. But when something caught his eye and he called out the command, his men were always ready, weapons and cannons primed for action. Just one word, and they came together like a well-oiled machine.

He put the spyglass away and looked across to the foredeck. John, the quartermaster, was overseeing some of the men scrubbing the deck, making sure nothing was missed. He was a stickler for getting things done but the men respected him completely.

Grimes and Callum were unraveling and repairing some rigging nearby, connecting the chains and tackle that controlled the masts and sails. They had thick ropes laid across the deck which they then attached to big metal pulleys. Although the men were experienced, it was advisable to keep your distance until the pulleys were re-affixed. They were heavy and if one swung loose, it could do a person a lot of damage.

He was just thinking of returning to his cabin, when a movement to the left caught his eye. He turned his head to see one of the young lads walking directly towards Grimes. He frowned. What in God's name was he doing in that vicinity? Someone should be supervising him. He spat an oath and quickly descended the quarterdeck.

Sophia gripped the wooden box tightly in her hands as she searched for the chicken coop. Smithy had said it was easy to find, but that was all very well if you knew where to look. The ship was large and all she had found so far were wooden crates, big coils of rope, large barrels secured with rope and several cannons. Continuing up the deck, she finally spied the evasive coop. She might have missed it except for the fact that one of the chickens stuck its head out through the bars.

There were several men working on ropes. She just had to get past them and she'd be able to collect the eggs for Seamus. She looked down at the heavy ropes; they were laid out all over the deck in front of her so she would have to be careful where she trod. She lifted her foot to begin stepping over them when one of the men, realising she was there, looked at her in horror and shouted out, "Get outta the way!"

Before she had a chance to react, she felt a large hand snake around her waist, and suddenly, her feet left the ground and she was whisked out of the way, just as a large metal pulley swung directly in front of her. It was so close, she felt the draft of air assail her cheeks.

She gasped with shock, only then realising what danger she had been in. "Oh my!"

"Oh my, indeed." growled a deep voice. Sophia stiffened immediately. Oh no! It was Jack. Oh, lord. She couldn't hide now.

She suddenly found herself turned around in his arms and the reprimand he was going to give her died the instant he looked at her.

They stared at each other silently. One, wishing the ground would open up, the other, wondering if he was hallu- cinating. "Sophia?" Jack finally said.

"P-pardon?" Sophia decided to pretend she had no idea

what he was talking about and lowered her eyelashes. "My name is Isaac, Captain."

When he didn't respond, she tried to wriggle out of his arms, but he held her fast. Her green eyes flashed to his and she could clearly see her ruse hadn't worked. His jaw had set tight and his expression was one of annoyance.

Grimes stepped forward. "Sorry, Cap'n. We didn't see the lad. 'E's lucky to be alive, that thing could've taken 'is 'ead clean off."

"It's not your fault, Grimes. The lad shouldn't have been anywhere near you. Someone's head is going to roll." He finally released Sophia, helping her upright, not taking his eyes off her. "*You* are going to join me in my quarters."

Sophia thought about disobeying but then decided she had little choice but to go with him. Perhaps it was for the best. Once she told him her intention was to join her brother, then surely, he would help her.

Jack led Sophia into his cabin and sat her down on the sofa. He stared at her for a long moment, still not quite believing what his eyes were showing him. She had thought to deceive him by coming on board dressed as a boy, but those vivid green eyes were unforgettable.

She stared up at him, clearly nervous now she had been discovered.

He leaned back against his desk and crossed his arms over his chest. "Firstly, how did you get onboard my ship and, secondly, why?"

"I had to escape from my father and… and I thought if I dressed as a boy, it would be a good way of stowing away on board a ship." She raised her chin a bit. "I didn't know it was your ship and I certainly didn't know you were a captain."

"So you just decided to stow away on a random ship that could take you off to God knows where?" he said sternly. "Do you know how dangerous it is on a ship like this? You could've been knocked senseless just now if that pulley had caught you! Not to mention what some of the crew might have done if they'd discovered you were a woman!"

He watched her fidget uneasily and her plump little bottom lip thrust out with vexation. She raised her chin and said, "Well, no one warned me about the pulley. Don't blame me."

"Oh, I am blaming you. You shouldn't even be here." He stood up and walked over to her. "Well, one thing is for sure. You cannot remain here."

Her eyes flashed to his. "What're you going to do?"

"Take you back home."

Sophia jumped up and balled her fists by her side. "You can't do that! I won't go!"

"You have no choice. My decision is made. I understand what sort of man your father is, but running away on a pirate ship is not the remedy. I will take you back, and when I return from Portsmouth, we'll meet up and find a solution together."

"I'm not going back."

"Sophia, don't defy me," he warned her. "You *will* go back."

She took no notice. "Fie, I'll take my chances overboard if that happens!"

Her lips were set tight and he could see the steely determination in her eyes.

"I don't know what has happened between your father and you, but this is not the solution. Do as I say and I promise to help you on my return."

"I don't believe you. Please just take me with you to

Portsmouth or wherever the next port of call is. I can send word to my brother."

"Leave you in a strange place on your own? It's more than foolish. No, Sophia. You're going home."

She went to say something and he stilled her with his hand. "Not another word!"

"Fie, you are pigheaded. I thought you gallant, but you're far from it."

"Enough!" He leaned down, putting his face a few inches away from hers. "Carry on in that vein and I'll put you straight over my knee."

He noted her eyes widened a fraction. "You would spank me?"

He nodded. "Whether you are crew or a stowaway, this is my ship, and my command is law. So, enough with your insults. Behave until we return, or else."

Her mouth fell open slightly. "You cannot speak to me like that!"

"I just did. So heed my words. You will remain in here until I return." He strode out of the cabin, and after locking the door securely behind himself, he disappeared up onto the deck. The sooner they changed course, the better. As much as he commiserated with Sophia, having her on board his ship could cause all sorts of problems. How would a refined woman like her cope with the skirmishes she would encounter? To his crew, it was all part of a normal day's work, danger was written in their DNA, but to a petite, little plantation owner's daughter? He shook his head. No, she was safer on land, but he would uphold his promise to help her when he returned from England, and Jack always kept his word.

Sophia waited until he had gone before jumping up and running over to the big lattice windows. The vast ocean stared back at her, blue and empty, no other vessels in sight.

What could she do? She certainly couldn't jump overboard as she had threatened. She wasn't that stupid, although she was nearly that desperate. But, no. She knew she wouldn't survive, and as much as she hated her father, she loved life too much to give it up.

She turned her back on the horizon and surveyed the cabin, her eyes darting around whilst wondering what she could do. There was a small door to her left, so she ran over and opened it, finding it to be a small privy room. Quickly, she stepped inside and, closing the door, turned the small key and locked herself in. Let him try to get her off the ship now!

Whilst she waited, she bit her bottom lip. Would he actually carry out his threat and spank her? She clenched her buttocks, anticipating his large hands falling on her silky skin. It sent a thrill running through her and she immediately admonished herself. What on earth was she thinking!

She heard someone's footsteps as they entered the cabin and kept still, listening hard to see if it was Jack. The privy handle turned and she watched it with big eyes.

"Sophia! Unlock this door."

It was most definitely Jack.

"No!" she snapped angrily. "Not until you promise not to take me back home," she demanded.

"I'll ask one more time, and then woe betide you if you disobey me. Open. This. Door."

"No!"

For a moment, there was silence and she was sure she heard him mutter an oath. The next minute, there was a loud bang, the door handle fell to the floor and the door itself was thrown open with such force that the hinges nearly came off.

Sophia gasped, but before she could even think of escape, a strong hand encircled her wrist and she found herself being unceremoniously hauled towards the sofa.

"Noooo!" she cried.

But her words fell on deaf ears. She was promptly thrown over his lap when he sat down on the sofa and his hand fell onto her quivering bottom, making a resounding slap that reverberated around the cabin.

Sophia shrieked and tried to wriggle off, but his tight grip kept her firmly pinned to his solid thighs. His hand came down in quick succession, smack after smack, and no amount of wailing or protests stopped him.

His deep voice admonished her throughout, and she was left in no doubt about her error of judgment. When he told her to obey him, he meant every word.

Her bottom began to feel like a furnace and she wondered if she would ever be able to sit down again in comfort.

Finally, with one last ringing slap on her sensitive posterior, he released her. She scrambled up and hopped around in front of him, holding both hands on her burning backside and throwing him a look of indignance.

"How could you do that?" she moaned.

"Very easily," he replied. "And I will have no hesitation in doing so again. Heed me well, Sophia." He stood up, towering over her, and she looked up at him, her bottom lip pouting. "Now, sit down and behave."

"Sit down? How can I sit down when you have made it impossible!"

His lip twitched at the corner with mirth and her eyes narrowed angrily. He put his hand on her shoulder and said with amusement, "Well then, it may behoove you to obey me next time."

Sophia thought about saying something but then decided against it. If she wanted to stay on board ship, then she was going to have to get on his good side. So, as hard as that seemed, she was going to have to behave. It would take a while to turn the ship about, so in that time, she had to win him over. But how?

Chapter 4

JACK STUDIED Sophia's face and recognised a scheming mind when he saw it. He laughed silently to himself. She had no idea how transparent she was.

He took a seat at his desk and placed his booted feet on the surface, leaning back in his chair so he could scrutinize her. She was gingerly sitting on the edge of the sofa, clearly uncomfortable but still determined to get her own way.

Her petite little bottom had fit perfectly over his lap, and spanking her pert, rounded derriere had certainly not been a chore.

He studied her openly. Would it be such a problem to take her with him? She certainly had a lot more spirit than he had first thought and didn't appear to be as timid as when they had first met. In fact, it would seem she had a bit of a temper.

Her father was an odious man, and even though he had said he would take her home, it didn't really sit well with him. But the idea of taking her on such a dangerous journey was also not to his liking.

He thrummed his fingers on the polished desk. She had

obviously run away for a reason and perhaps he should let her explain. She didn't strike him as someone who did something without a good reason.

He would order John to drop anchor before making a final decision.

Standing up, he made his way over to the door and said to Sophia, "I'll return shortly and we'll have a discussion." He pointed his finger at her. "I'm going to lock you in because I don't trust you not to run away."

Sophia stared back at him silently, her face brooding. Shaking his head, he left the cabin. She was one stubborn little madam.

Hearing the key turn in the lock, Sophia jumped to her feet and stomped around the cabin, every now and then rubbing her sore bottom to ease the discomfort. He was mean to spank her so and she would tell him when he returned.

She looked out to the horizon, noting the gentle waves on the vast expanse of ocean in front of her. It was unfair. She had come this far, and there was no way on this earth that she was returning home. No way. None.

Her lips tightened angrily. It was so frustrating, and she wasn't going to allow Jack to control her. Her temper rose and she looked around for something to throw at him. Maybe that would make him take notice.

A few moments later, Jack unlocked the door of his quarters and stepped inside, neatly dodging the jug of water that Sophia hurled at him.

"What the hell?" he exclaimed. "Is this how you treat the captain of the ship? You are a spoiled brat."

Sophia glared at him, her chest heaving and her whole demeanour one of rebellion.

He looked directly at her and said sharply, "Do you need another lesson in manners, Sophia?"

One more word from her, and he would have no hesitation in throwing her back over his knee. He noted her eyes lowered to the floor for a moment, and when she raised them back to his, she seemed a little less rebellious. His warning seemed to have worked.

Suddenly, her face crumpled and she raised her hands to cover her face. "I can't go back. Please, please do not make me." Her voice ended on a sob and Jack rolled his eyes. A woman's tears never failed to move him, and now was no different.

Muttering an oath, he strode towards her and cradled her to his chest. "I think you need to explain to me what happened." Gently, he led her over to the sofa and sat her down next to him, his hands cupping hers. "What's so bad that you felt the need to run away?"

Sophia looked at him through tear-stained lashes and began to explain about her father accusing her of stealing and his ultimate decision to send her to a reform school. She also told him about her twin brother's aim to buy a house for them both in the near future. She omitted the fact that Isaac was also in the same trade as he was—piracy. She felt it was a secret too far. So she just told him he worked on the *Nonsuch* merchant ship.

When she finished, Jack gave an audible sigh. "How old are you, Sophia?"

"Twenty-three."

He shook his head. "Yet your father thinks it acceptable

to send you to a reform school. He is a fool." His thumb caressed her hand and Sophia found it hard to concentrate. She looked down, noting how her hands were so small compared to his.

His next words made her ear prick up. "I *will* take you to the next port but this all depends."

She angled her head. "On what?"

"Whether you can behave or not." He looked over at the pewter jug lying on its side on the floor. "No more missiles, for one thing, and you are to obey my every command. This is a dangerous place for a man, let alone a woman, so I would have your promise that if I tell you to do something, you'll heed me."

Sophia nodded emphatically. She'd agree to anything at the moment to get her own way. It didn't mean she'd keep her word.

"Very well. You can remain on board until we reach Bordeaux. From there, we can send word to your brother." His brow furrowed. "Where is he at the moment?"

"He's on his way to Jamaica."

Jack rubbed his forehead. "Jamaica is in entirely the other direction."

"Oh, yes… but I can stay in Bordeaux and send word to him," she said in a small voice.

"You haven't thought this through properly, have you?" He shot her a look of exasperation. "Where are you going to stay in Bordeaux? Do you have enough money? How will you get word to your brother?"

Her face fell and a look of despondency took over.

Jack thought hard for a moment and then gave a resigned shrug. "Well, I guess we can change course. It will only delay us by about two weeks and we might find a ship or two to plunder along the way. Always a bonus." He gave her a resigned smile and she almost swooned. He was so handsome. Despite his recent treatment of her, it didn't quell her attraction to him. He was so strong and masculine—something she responded to without question.

He stood up and pointed at the bed. "You can have the bed. I'll take the couch."

"I'll sleep in here? With you?" Her stomach flipped.

"Of course. I can't have you sleeping elsewhere. I intend to make sure you travel safely and if that means you taking my bed, then so be it." He smiled at her. "Don't worry. I may be a pirate, but I'm also a gentleman."

Sophia felt a blush suffuse her cheeks. "Gentlemen don't spank ladies!" she blurted out.

Jack raised an eyebrow. "Oh, they do. When a lady misbehaves, it's a gentleman's duty to admonish her."

She stared at him, unsure whether to argue further and wondering if that might hamper his decision to let her stay on board. She opted to keep her thoughts to herself for now and said, "Won't it inconvenience you if I stay in here?"

"Not at all. I'd rather have you in my sight than down below disguised as a boy. Lord knows what sort of language you've encountered already or what shenanigans you've witnessed. This ramshackle lot can be rather rambunctious when they want to be."

Sophia bit her bottom lip and then giggled. "I'd expect nothing less."

"Indeed." He smiled back and then looked her up and down. "Did you bring any other clothes with you?"

She nodded and told him about her carpet bag which was now in the shared cabin with Smithy.

"I'll have someone fetch it. I trust you not to leave the cabin whilst I'm gone?" He gave her a stern look, one eyebrow raised.

She shook her head. "No, I promise."

When he'd left the cabin, Sophia smiled to herself. This

was turning out better than planned. The ship was only about two days behind *Sunfire*, so hopefully, she would encounter her brother within days. Freedom was within her grasp.

Jack returned with her carpet bag, and after ordering some hot water from Smithy, he left her to her ablutions.

Half an hour later, Sophia felt like a new person. Washed and cleansed, her hair neatly braided and back in her feminine attire, she felt more than ready to face the world. The knowledge that Jack had agreed to her remaining on board his ship, made her whole situation better. She could meet up with Isaac and then start a whole new life away from her tyrannical father.

She smiled to herself, remembering Smithy's face when Jack had introduced her as Sophia, rather than the little lad called Isaac. His jaw had nearly fallen onto the floor when she'd taken off her headscarf and her blonde locks had tumbled down her back. The news would be circulating all around the ship now. She just hoped they had no objections to a woman being on board. Her brother had told her that some of his own men often spoke about bad omens when a woman came on board. Although he had noted, it didn't pertain to a comely wench when the need arose.

Oh, well, it was only for a couple of days. If they didn't like it, that was their problem! This was a means to an end and she could endure anything.

The door opened and Jack returned. He stopped for a moment and she saw admiration in his eyes as he looked her up and down.

"Now, that's better. How do you feel?"

"Refreshed." She grinned. "I truly appreciate what you're doing for me." Her green eyes sparkled happily.

He walked over and, lifting her hand, kissed the soft skin. "Did anyone ever tell you that you have beautiful eyes?"

A surge of heat ripped through Sophia's slender body at his touch and his words made her catch her breath. He had such an effect on her that she found herself tongue-tied.

His gaze lingered for a moment and then, gently, he let her hand drop. "I've ordered some food for us. You have no objection to eating together?"

Sophia shook her head. "No, of course not." It would be interesting to find out more about him. After all, he now knew quite a lot about her but she knew hardly anything about him.

A little while later, Smithy arrived with a tray of food. He looked slightly embarrassed when he saw her, and after he had placed the tray on the table, he stepped back a bit. "I'm rightly sorry, miss, if I might 'ave said somat wrong to ye before like. None of us thought ye was a woman. If I might say, ye did a good disguise."

"I, too, am sorry to have duped you," she explained, "but I had to get away from my father. I knew of no other way."

He smiled. "Well, if ye need anythin', just let me know and I'll be 'appy to 'elp."

Sophia thanked him, and when he'd left the cabin, Jack smiled. "Haven't seen him looking so chipper in years! Reckon you've made a friend for life there."

He proceeded to serve them the food, making sure she had a substantial portion of everything on the tray. She didn't argue, as the chicken looked delicious, along with the potatoes and carrots. He pushed a plate towards her and then poured her a glass of red wine.

She ate with relish, realising how hungry she was. In between forkfuls of the simple yet delicious meal, she asked

Jack about his life. He revealed he was one of three brothers and that *Blythe Spirit* was owned equally by all of them, including their father. As far as the authorities were concerned, he was part owner of a family run business, importing wines and spirits in England. But his older brother, Logan, had been fed up with the taxes levied on their business and had decided to take to piracy, plundering privateers who had stolen off others. It had proved lucrative.

Logan had met his wife two years ago and had decided to remain on land. So Jack had stepped in as captain.

He smiled at her. "And I can truthfully say, I've never looked back."

"You do seem very content," she remarked. But then she knew how much her brother loved piracy so it figured. She finished her wine and yawned, covering her mouth with her hand. "Oh, excuse me. I think today is catching up on me."

"I think you need to go to bed."

He stood up and walked over to the bed, pulling down the coverlet. It looked so inviting. "I have to go up on deck so I'll leave you to prepare for sleep. I'll try not to disturb you when I return." He looked at the table. "I shall clear the table myself tonight so Smithy won't enter the cabin."

When he'd left, Sophia quickly changed into a nightgown she had brought with her and slipped beneath the coverlet, snuggling into the very soft mattress. It felt odd to be sleeping in Jack's bed, but she was so tired that sleep soon overcame her and any misgivings were soon forgotten.

Jack woke up in the morning and stretched his legs, wondering why he didn't feel as comfortable as usual. And then he remembered he was on the couch. Opening his eyes, he sat up and looked over to the bed, where he found his little stowaway still slumbering peacefully.

His expression softened. Even in sleep, she was beautiful. Tendrils of hair had escaped her plait and were framing her petite features. His gaze moved downwards, noting the swell of her breasts and the curve of her hips as she lay on her side. He felt his cock twitch in response and wondered how she would feel if he joined her. He raised an eyebrow, knowing she would most probably launch something at him.

He had learned a lot about her during their dinner last night. Far from the timid, shy girl he had first encountered, she seemed to have a strong will and a determined mind. The very fact that she had dared launch something at him, meant she possessed somewhat of a stubborn nature. Who would dare throw a jug at a pirate captain?

But he was glad for it. Without it, she may not have fared so well living with such a tyrant of a father. She had even revealed that she could handle a sword, her brother having taught her from a young age. It made him wonder what sort of man her brother was. He was obviously of good character, for he was saving to buy them a house together. Perhaps one day they would meet.

Smiling, he slipped from beneath the covers and, on bare feet, padded over to the cabin door. Wrenching it open, he hollered up the corridor, "Hot water, if you please, Smithy!"

"Oh!" He heard a brief shriek, and then whirling around, realised he had, out of habit, called out his usual morning order and in the process woken her up.

"Forgive me, Sophia. I didn't mean to startle you."

She was clutching the covers and staring at him with her intense green eyes and her face still flushed with sleep. She gulped and shook her head. "I forgot where I was for a moment." He noticed she lowered her eyes and her colour deepened. It appeared his attire, or rather, lack of, was making her uncomfortable. Dressed only in his long shirt, he surmised it would be a little daunting for a lady.

"I had no intention of waking you so abruptly." He smiled apologetically and quickly reaching for his britches, began to get dressed.

A knock came on the door and he barked out, "Come!" allowing Smithy to enter with a jug and bowl of hot water. A young lad placed a tray of breakfast on the table. He thanked them, and when they had gone, he turned to Sophia and said, "I'll leave you to wash and dress. When I return, we can take breakfast together."

He quickly left the cabin and headed down to the galley to get some more hot water for his own use and left Sophia with some privacy. He smiled, remembering her tousled hair and sleepy eyes. She was beautiful even when she had just awoken. Oh, how he would like to share that bed with her, watch as her eyes fluttered open and claim her lips in a hot, searing kiss.

Jack shifted uncomfortably. He had been too long without a woman, it would seem. Something he would have to rectify at the next port of call. An image of Sophia's pert little bottom draped over his lap came into his mind and he groaned aloud, trying to dismiss the image from his mind.

When he ordered the water for his morning wash, he told Smithy to make sure it was cold! Anything to help dampen his desire.

Later that morning…

Standing on the deck, Jack sucked in a lungful of salty sea air and gave a satisfied sigh. With the sun shining and hardly a cloud in the sky, it never failed to raise his spirits.

Plus the fact that he had a gorgeous woman in his cabin. Indeed, it was a beautiful day to be alive.

Grimes interrupted his thoughts by calling out, "Sail ho!" from the crow's nest.

Jack immediately raised his spyglass and scanned the horizon for activity. In the distance, he could make out the vessel Grimes had seen. It seemed to be heading in their direction. At the moment, it was too hard to tell its size or nationality.

"Maintain our course, John," he told the quartermaster. "We'll see if she's worth plundering or not."

A little while later, Jack raised his spyglass again and moved it along the ship's hull, searching out the vessel's name. Suddenly, he found it, and immediately, his jaw tightened. *Sunfire*!

He'd been seeking revenge on this ship for months. John noticed his anger and asked, "What is it, Cap'n?"

"It's the damned *Sunfire*."

"That bastard!" he spat. "Scoundrel bloody well stole off us."

"Damned right he did, and now he's going to pay. Ready the men!"

Sunfire had caught him at a disadvantage last time. Docked at Port Nassau, Jack had business on shore and whilst he and John were away negotiating the sale of their current wares, *Sunfire's* crew had taken the opportunity to attack. Cautiously and silently, they had climbed aboard and taken his crew by surprise.

Jack had returned to his ship to find mayhem. Some of the crew lay wounded and the rest had been tied up. Their recent booty, that he had negotiated so hard to sell, had been stolen from under his very nose.

Jack's eyes narrowed angrily. This time, the cocky bastard would regret coming anywhere near *Blythe Spirit*!

Jack walked over towards his quarters and, descending the steps, opened the door to his cabin. Sophia was sitting on the window seat, reading one of his books, a look of serenity on her face. Jack didn't want to be the one to tell her that all hell was about to be let loose, but it had to be done.

"Sophia?"

She glanced up from her book and shot him a small smile, waiting for him to speak. It was at that moment that she seemed to become aware of the noise on deck. He watched as a small frown marred her brow.

"We are about to attack another ship. " He held up his hand. "Don't be alarmed, just remain in here, out of sight. Lock the door behind me and open it for no one except me or John, do you understand?"

Sophia jumped up from her seat, the book falling to the floor in her haste, her eyes wide. "Attack?"

"Yes." He walked over to the wall and lifted down one of the swords. "You say you are adept at sword fighting, so use this if necessary. It might be your only protection." He laid it down on the desk.

Her face paled and she swayed slightly. "But—"

"Sophia, this is a pirate ship. It was your choice to come on board, now is not the time to have regrets."

"I know that, but what if you get harmed?"

He frowned. "You're concerned for me?"

She nodded, slightly embarrassed at the revelation. "Well, yes. It's only natural."

He stared at her for a moment and was going to respond when suddenly the silence was filled with gunfire. He immediately shot into action. "Do as I say and lock this door!"

Instantly, he was gone. Sophia rushed over to the door and slammed it shut, turning the key in the lock for safety. Turning around, she leaned against the heavy wood, her heart racing and her eyes wide with fear.

Good lord. She had often wondered what it would be like to be on *Sunfire* and experience a battle aboard ship, and now it was actually happening, she wondered if she hadn't underestimated such an experience.

Sunfire was romping up towards them at quite a speed; even in the light breeze, there was a white wave under her sharp bows. Jack glanced up to make sure that the merchant flag was still displayed. He wanted to lure *Sunfire* onward and let her think they were just a merchant vessel.

The report of a gun and a puff of smoke came from the other ship as she dared to fire across *Blythe Spirit*'s bows again.

Jack's eyes narrowed with anger. Sunfire drew even nearer, her crew plainly visible now.

"Wait, men, wait," said Jack.

The ship was coming alongside when suddenly Jack bellowed, "Come on, men!"

He ran across the deck, grabbed a rope and flung himself across the gap, straight at the captain. If anyone was going to get the bastard, it was he. He fell with all his weight on the unfortunate man, clasped him round the shoulders, and fell with him to the deck. There were shouts and yells behind him as *Blythe Spirit*'s crew joined him. A rush of feet, a clatter and a clash. Jack easily overpowered the younger captain and soon had his hands tied behind his back.

Grimes was just striking down a man with his cutlass. Foster was heading forward towards the main cabin, waving a cutlass and yelling like a madman. Then it was all over; the astonished crew of the *Sunfire* was unable to lift a hand in their own defence. The ship was theirs.

Back on *Blythe Spirit,* Jack propelled the captain towards the main mast. "Tie him up," he ordered Grimes.

The young captain glared at him. "If you're going to kill me, do it now."

Jack shot him an evil smile. "In case it has escaped your notice, you're my prisoner. It's not the other way around. I shall decide what to do with you in a little while—once we have plundered your ship. I thought it would be nice for you to stay here and watch. Something you failed to allow me the courtesy of."

The captain curled his lip. "You cannot blame me for your shortcomings, sir."

Jack raised an eyebrow. "Shortcomings? Brave words for someone in your position."

The man was only young, and despite his bravado, he had a lot to learn. One was to keep his mouth shut, and the second was never to attack Jack's ship.

Sunfire's captain tried to struggle against his bonds and Jack laughed heartily. "Grimes' ropework is one of the best, you won't get out of that in a hurry."

Grimes grinned and peered right in the captain's face. "Ye better believe 'im. And even if ye do, I've got a cutlass 'ere that'll make sure ye don't get very far."

Satisfied that the captain was secured, Jack turned on his heel and called over to John, "Start the unloading, John. I'll join you in a moment."

Striding across the deck, he descended the short steps to his cabin and knocked on the door. He heard the key turn in the lock and the door opened instantly. Sophia stared at him with wide eyes, before stepping back and letting him pass.

Before she had a chance to say anything, he rounded on her. "What were you thinking?"

"Pardon?"

"Did I not specifically tell you to only open the door when you knew it was me?"

"B-but—"

"No buts. You never asked if it was me, did you? I could've been anyone." He placed his hand under her chin and raised her face to his. "I'm going to punish you for that later."

He watched her cheeks grow hot under his gaze, knowing what he had planned for her. Then her temper burst forth.

She twisted her chin out of his hand and snapped, "That is completely unfair! I knew it was you by your footsteps."

Jack folded his arms across his chest and shook his head. "No, you didn't. Don't lie, else your punishment will be prolonged."

She had the temerity to look a little shamefaced and lowered her gaze, before turning her back to him.

Smiling to himself, he immediately reached out and drew her against him and whispered in her ear, "Were you worried for me?"

"Hmmph! No." She bristled.

"Ah, you were. I know it. Well, as you can see, I am fine. We're the victors and the crew is already unloading *Sunfire*'s goods onto ours."

He felt her body go stiff, and extricating herself from his embrace, she whirled around and stared at him. "*Sunfire*? Did you say *Sunfire*?"

Jack nodded. "What of it?

Her eyes sparkled angrily. "The captain is my brother!"

Chapter 5

JACK STARED BACK at Sophia in amazement. "That low life little upstart is your brother?"

Sophia gasped, "How dare you call him that!"

His eyes darkened. "I dare call him anything I like. He stole off me and now I intend to make him pay."

"You are too conceited. He only does what you dare to do! You are both pirates who are cut from the same cloth."

"So you lied to me," he said accusingly. "You told me he worked on a merchant ship."

"It was necessary to lie at the time. It makes no difference now you know what he truly is."

He watched her stride to the door, and realising her intent, he quickly grabbed her arm. "Oh, no, you don't. You'll stay in here until I decide what to do with you."

"What do you mean?" she asked, trying to struggle free of his grip.

"It means exactly what I just said." He picked her up and sat her down on the bed. "Behave until I get back." She went to get up and he pointed his finger at her. "Sit!"

He watched her struggle with her emotions. It was

obvious she wanted to defy him, but she also knew the consequences of such an act. So, in the end, she just glared at him.

Leaving the cabin, he locked the door behind himself and ventured up on deck.

Sophia jumped up from the bed and paced the cabin when he'd left. How dare he keep her confined to quarters when her brother was so close. In fact, it was the very reason she was on board this ship in the first place. Ooh. He was so unreasonable.

She ran to the door and placed her ear against the wood, straining to hear his voice. But there was too much commotion to hear anything. Jack said they were unloading *Sunfire*'s goods—goods that would have given her more money in her quest to leave home. She placed her hands over her face. Good lord. Everything was going wrong!

Jack stood in front of Isaac, his legs astride, and gave him a hard stare. Isaac's temper hadn't diminished and Jack now knew where his twin sister got her temper from. Like peas in a pod.

"What are you staring at?" Isaac spat, his eyes blazing fire.

"I'd watch that mouth of yours if I were you," Jack warned him.

"Well, you aren't me, are you? Do you expect me just to remain silent whilst you plunder my ship?"

"You'd be silent if you knew what treasure I have of yours on board."

Isaac narrowed his eyes. "What do you mean? What treasure? Gold?"

Jack gave a low laugh. "Something far more precious than gold."

He watched as Isaac's expression changed a little, a smidgen of fear had crept in. Good, it would do the youngster well to learn to curb his tongue.

"What do you speak of? Tell me!" His voice held a note of desperation and Jack decided to put him out of his misery.

"Sophia. Your sister, I believe."

Isaac's jaw fell open. "You jest! How can she be here?"

"Oh, that's a long story, for another time. But, yes, she's here, and at this precise moment, she's in my cabin."

"I don't believe you!"

"Believe it or not. It makes no difference to me."

"If what you say is true, you'd better not have harmed her or I will—"

Jack interrupted him, "You will do what, exactly? I commend your bravery, but in your position, I would watch what I said."

Isaac stared back at him, his lips tight, his expression now a little guarded. "What do you intend to do with her?"

Jack thought hard for a few moments before replying. One sure way of making Isaac pay for his crimes was to keep Sophia with him. It would make him think twice before daring to attack *Blythe Spirit.*

"I'm going to take her as a prize," he announced, showing a smile that didn't quite reach his eyes.

"The devil, you are!"

"And how do you intend to stop me?" Jack inched nearer to him and stared into the same green eyes as his mischievous sister's. "We'll take your goods and then set you free. Think on it as an act of benevolence. And to guarantee your compliance, I will keep Sophia with me. Rest assured that she'll be well provided for. She's in no danger."

Isaac stared at him angrily. "And what does my sister have to say about this? What is she even doing on your ship?"

"Your sister will do as I tell her. I don't have time to reveal the full tale of why she's here but know this—it was her choice."

On that note, he turned on his heel and ignored the rest of Isaac's questions as his words were carried away by the wind.

Sophia was in high dudgeon when he returned, the colour high in her cheeks. "How's my brother? If you intend to harm him, I'll… I'll…"

"You'll do what, my sweet little firebrand?" He walked up to her and placed his hand on her chin, lowering his face until he was just inches away. "If you care for your brother, you'll behave."

In the depths of her emerald-green eyes, he could see the simmering anger but, admirably, she managed to contain it. With a low growl, he placed a hand against the small of her back and, drawing her against him, he claimed her lips for his own. She resisted at first, her body stiff with indignance, but then he felt her soften and she gave in to his passionate kiss. A few seconds later, she seemed to realise what she was doing and pulled away abruptly. Her hand flew up and slapped him around the face.

The sound reverberated around the cabin. Her eyes flashed angrily at him and she spat, "How dare you take advantage of me!"

Jack noted the quick rise and fall of her bosom. As much as she fought against him, he knew the attraction was mutual. He had known too many hellcats not to know what was behind all that bluster and blaze.

"On this occasion, I'll forgive you for such an act." He

advised her, "But you will never do so again, do you understand?"

The tension between them was palpable and it took all of Jack's resilience not to claim her lips again and make her surrender to him.

She raised her chin defiantly and asked, "Can I see him?"

"Yes, but before you do, you need to know that you won't be leaving with him. You are to remain here."

Her eyes showed confusion. "Why must I remain here? The whole reason I stowed away on your ship was to seek out my brother. Why are you stopping me?"

"I don't trust your brother. He has stolen from me before and he could easily order his ship to attack when I release him. So for now, you'll remain with me. It will ensure his compliance."

"But that's not fair!"

"Don't blame me for your brother's actions, Sophia."

For a moment, he thought she was going to start throwing things again, but maybe thinking better of it, she turned her back on him, her skirts swishing loudly in protest, and snarled, "I hate you!"

"No, you don't. You know as well as I do that your brother would think nothing of getting his revenge, were I to hand you over. So for now, you must remain here. You can accompany me on my voyage to England and I'll return you safely home in a few months. Or if you prefer not to go back to your father, then Isaac can meet you in Jamestown."

She whirled around again. "So I have to stay on this damned ship for several months?"

He nodded and couldn't help shooting her a smile. "Will it be that hard to endure?"

Sophia regarded Jack silently. Her heart was racing for so many reasons, one being the fact that he had just kissed her. For a moment, she had succumbed to the delicious passion that he stirred within her breast, but when she had come to her senses, she had been annoyed with herself. How could she give in to her feelings when her poor brother was being held captive by the very man who thought he could take what wasn't his!

Her eyes searched his face. His look was intense. Did he want to keep her on his ship for his own selfish reasons, or was her brother truly such a massive threat to him.

She needed to speak with Isaac and see for herself.

"Let me speak with my brother."

"Very well, but the outcome will be the same."

Sophia was dismayed to see her brother tied up against the mast and her eyes shimmered with tears on seeing him. How dare Jack treat him like this. A tear slipped unbidden down her cheek as she stepped forward to greet him.

"Sophia!" He searched her face for signs of harm and found none. "What on earth are you doing on this ship? I only left you two days ago. What happened?"

"Father found our stash of money and accused me of stealing off him. He had organised for me to go to a reform school for six months. So I ran away." She wiped her tears away with her hand and tried to be brave.

"Bastard!" His lips thinned with anger and frustration.

Sophia's heart went out to him. "My intention was to somehow get a message to you and meet up. But it hasn't worked out that way." She glanced at Jack, to find him scrutinising her. She raised her chin and said to Isaac, "Please don't worry about me, though. Despite current circumstances, I still prefer being here than there and we can meet up again soon. At least I have escaped Father."

Isaac turned his gaze on Jack. "If you harm one hair on her head, I promise you'll suffer."

"I assure you that I have no intention of harming her. She'll accompany me on my voyage to England and will be treated with all due respect. You can meet me at Archer's Hope in mid-September, where she'll be returned to you."

Isaac curled his lip. "I don't get a choice, do I?"

Sophia listened to her brother, and her temper began to rise, her tears diminishing. She hated seeing her brother rendered so powerless.

Jack shook his head. "None whatsoever." He grinned confidently. "But you do have my word that her safety will be a priority." He turned to Sophia. "Now bid your brother adieu, for I intend to set sail."

She responded darkly, her eyes blazing violent rage. "No, I shall not."

They both looked at her, Isaac, realising his sister's temper was about to erupt and Jack, wondering what she was going to do.

Callum, standing nearby, whispered to Grimes, "Did I "ear that right. Did she just say no to Lucky Jack?"

Grimes nodded. "This ain't gonna end well."

"What do you mean 'no'?" Jack asked her, his voice low.

"Exactly that. I'm going with my brother. It is not for you to decide where I can and cannot go. I want to go back where I belong."

He raised an eyebrow. "I am afraid you may not."

Sophia stomped her foot angrily. "This is unfair. Isaac will promise not to attack your ship, won't you?" She swung her head around to look at her brother.

Isaac took a deep breath and closed his eyes for a

moment before opening them again and, staring hard at Jack, replied, "For my sister, I can promise."

Jack laughed. "And you expect me to believe you? Do you think I was born yesterday?" He grabbed Sophia's arm and began to lead her away. "Come on. Get back to my cabin and stay there."

Sophia struggled and tried to pull away from him. "Why should I do as you say?"

"I am the captain of this ship and you are taking my orders. That's why."

She called out to her brother, "Isaac!"

Jack muttered an oath, and in one swoop, he gathered her up into his arms, ignoring her protests, and threw her straight over his shoulder.

"Put me down! It's not fair!" Sophia shrieked angrily.

"I gave you the chance to say goodbye and you chose to have a tantrum. That was your choice. Now you're going to be confined to my quarters." His patience was now hanging on by a thread.

"You lout! You oaf!" Sophia pummelled his back, but her small fists made little impact, and within minutes, she was back in his cabin.

He sat her down and pointed a finger in her face. "Behave!"

"Fie, I shall not! You cannot keep me like this!"

"You're my captive, and as my captive, you're in no situation to make demands."

Sophia spluttered with anger and threw herself at him, pounding her small fists into his hard chest. He captured her hands and turned her around so her back was moulded against him.

She felt his hot breath on her ear, and despite her predicament, a thrill shot up her spine. "Now, now, my little spitfire, I suggest you accept your fate and cease fighting me. You'll find life a lot easier if you do."

She cursed and immediately kicked backwards, incensed at being held against her will. He sucked in a breath as his shin began to throb with pain. His patience suddenly reached the end of its tether.

"Let me go!" she demanded again, "I want to go with my brother!" Her voice ended on a high note as she felt herself upended over one of his large thighs, the wooden floor staring her in the face. Her skirts were promptly thrown over her back. Her mouth made a small O of surprise, and when she felt a searing pain on her bottom, she knew Jack had just lost his patience.

His hand came down in quick succession, spanking her hard upon her soft flesh, barely protected by her thin bloomers. Her face screwed up when her backside began to smart with pain.

"You don't make demands of a pirate captain, Sophia."

Sophia shrieked and tried to wriggle off his thigh, but he was too strong. In fact, she had forgotten how strong he really was. His arm held her tight against his waist, and no matter how much she shrieked or pummelled his legs, Jack continued spanking her bottom until she was whimpering and truly regretting making any sort of demand.

Finally, he released his grip and she sprang up as though burned, her hands quickly rubbing her backside to alleviate the throbbing pain.

"When will you learn to obey me?" he asked her.

Sophia's bottom lip pouted, but this time she refrained from giving him any back chat. She didn't want to receive any more smacks on her bottom. It was tender enough already.

He regarded her sternly. "I suggest you remain calm whilst I'm gone. If I find anything thrown around the room or thrown at me when I return, I will continue where I left off. Do you understand?"

Sophia nodded. He stared at her for a few moments and then strode to the door. As the door closed behind him, she heard the key turn in the lock, and throwing herself on the bed, she gave in to tears. Tears of frustration, that her life was being controlled by such a devil.

Jack surveyed the last of the crates being unloaded from *Sunfire* and smiled with satisfaction. He had far more than Isaac had stolen off him. That would teach the lad a well-earned lesson.

John joined him by the railing. "Should get a fair price for this lot, Cap'n. Reckon he won't bother us anytime in the future."

"Hopefully, he'll stick to ships more his size. Privateers, not pirates, eh?" He walked over to where Isaac was still secured. "So, Captain, do I have your assurance you'll be on your way without trouble?"

Isaac, still simmering with anger, replied, "You know I have no choice."

Jack smiled easily. "So, we're agreed. You'll be released back to your crew shortly and we'll be on our way. The damage to your ship shouldn't take long to fix, but that all depends on your crew." He looked across to *Sunfire's* deck, noting the crew tied up and rendered incapable of retaliation. It would take Isaac a while to release them all from their bonds and get the ship seaworthy enough to return even one volley, let alone embark on a full scale attack. He looked back at Isaac. "Mid-September, we'll meet at Archer's Hope."

He didn't wait for a response but, with a nod to Grimes

to release the prisoner, Jack strode up onto the foredeck in preparation to leave.

The wind was picking up and now was as good a time as any to set sail. Bellowing out orders, it didn't take long to weigh anchor and get the sails hoisted, the men swarming all over them with practised ease. They were promptly under-way, catching the wind to their advantage and leaving *Sunfire* in their wake.

That evening…

Jack watched Sophia from across the table. Her lips were pursed and it was obvious she was still angry with him. He supposed he wouldn't be very happy in her position, but at the same time, she had to realise her brother's previous actions against him had given rise to this very moment.

Her plate was still empty and she hadn't served herself any of the delicious food that Smithy had served them.

He pushed a platter towards her. "Potatoes? Bread and cheese?" She ignored him. "You're not eating."

"I'd rather starve!"

"I suppose a little fasting won't harm," he remarked, shooting her a smile, "besides, it might improve your manners."

Her eyes flashed angrily. "Manners? What would you know about manners!"

"Plenty." He stood up and pushed the other two platters towards her. "I'm going up on deck. I suggest you take this time to eat something. Starving yourself won't help."

Sophia folded her arms across her chest and looked away, raising her chin in defiance.

Shrugging nonchalantly, Jack left her to her own devices. Maybe once she had eaten something, her good humour would return, and time alone would surely make her realise that spending time with him was not such a bad thing. After all, he was Lucky Jack. He never usually had problems with women, even hellions surrendered to his charms and good looks.

He smiled to himself. Yes, all she needed was time.

Chapter 6

SOPHIA EYED the food platters in front of her and tried her damnedest to resist. But the delicious smells wafted up, and eyeing the door to make sure Jack wasn't coming back, she quickly reached for a chicken leg.

Taking a great bite, she chewed on the food, closing her eyes with bliss. She was starving. Before long, the chicken was devoured and she threw the stripped bone on the plate. Reaching for the jug, she poured herself a large goblet of red wine, smacking her lips when she tasted the smooth and velvety beverage.

After polishing off over half, she could feel her body beginning to mellow. Letting out a long sigh, she thought about her predicament. She was stuck on this ship with Jack, whether she liked it or not. And it was going to be for a long time.

It was so frustrating. She had been so near to her goal of being with her brother, and yet Jack had thwarted her attempts to do so. She should hate him, but she didn't. No, her feelings went much deeper.

She had had no idea that her brother had previously encountered Jack's ship and brazenly stolen off him. Good lord. What a predicament. But one thing was for sure—she would far rather be on Jack's ship than at home with her bastard of a father. A shudder ripped through her as she thought of home.

What would she do when her time with Jack was up and he returned her to her hometown? She could only hope that, by then, Issac would have made enough money for them to buy their own home, for one thing was sure, she would never live at Thorn Creek tobacco plantation ever again.

Throwing the last of the red wine down her throat, she slammed the goblet on the table and walked over to the bed, suddenly feeling very weary. Shrugging off her dress and bloomers, she sat down on the edge of the bed and pulled off her boots and stockings. Clad only in her shift, she crawled under the covers and settled on her side, hugging the soft blanket tightly as her eyes fluttered closed and she succumbed to sleep.

It was late when Jack finally returned to his quarters, having made sure they had put plenty of distance between his ship and *Sunfire*.

He entered the cabin quietly, so as not to disturb Sophia should she be sleeping. Closing the door, he saw her slumbering form in the dim glow from the lanterns. The sea was calm and with half the sails lowered, *Blythe Spirit* was slipping along at a nice, steady pace, creating only a gentle rocking motion. An easy environment to sleep in.

He sat down on a chair and pulled off his boots before reaching for a goblet. His eyes fell on the discarded chicken bone and he smiled to himself. There was hardly anything of the petite little firebrand, so it heartened him to see that she had at least eaten something.

Pouring himself some wine, he downed it in one go, smacking his lips with appreciation at the fine vintage. Made all the finer as it had cost him nothing. A wicked smile broke out on his handsome face. If there was one good thing about piracy, it was the knowledge of getting one over on the customs men and the government. A loss of taxes for their greedy coffers and a win for the common man.

His gaze moved to Sophia, noting the steady rise and fall of her chest as she slumbered peacefully in his bed. The temptation to join her was strong. He hadn't held a woman in a while and envisaged her warm, soft feminine form beneath the covers. She was a true beauty and possessed the fire and spirit that he admired.

She had seemed so coy and demure when he had first encountered her in Jamestown. He raised an eyebrow and smirked. Yet she had revealed herself to be quite the firebrand. What a temper! But he had ways of curbing that with a sound spanking on her plump, round bottom.

His loins responded as a wave of desire washed over him. Shifting uncomfortably in his seat, he tried to quell his thoughts. It wasn't easy.

Suddenly, Sophia whimpered. Jack's eyes shot to hers. Was she in pain? She whimpered again and gave what sounded like a sob. Immediately, Jack rushed over to look at her, peering into her face to see what was wrong. He quickly realised that she was still asleep and appeared to be having a nightmare. He pulled a face. No doubt, it was about him. She went quiet again and the frown on her brow diminished.

Walking over to the couch, he undressed down to his long shirt and reached for the folded coverlet preparing himself for sleep, but an unearthly scream suddenly filled the air. He whirled around to find Sophia sitting up in bed, her eyes wide with terror.

He rushed over and looked at her. She was staring straight ahead, and amazingly, she still seemed to be asleep. Her chest was heaving and she was clearly in a state of fright. Whatever her nightmare was about, it didn't seem to be going away. He sat down next to her and gently pulled her against his chest, hoping that his presence would somehow comfort her. It seemed to work, for she snuggled into him, her eyes closing and her breathing beginning to calm. He placed his cheek against her hair and closed his eyes, breathing in her floral scent. She was so small and vulnerable that he felt a sudden urge to protect her. Her father would never protect her, that was certain. What she needed was a husband and a secure future. His eyes sprung open. Was he offering himself for the job? No! What was he thinking? He wasn't ready for marriage.

His thoughts turned to his brother, Logan. He had given up a life of piracy for his bride. But did he want to do the same? He thought hard. No, he didn't. He loved every minute of life on *Blythe Spirit* and he couldn't envisage a life on land. Not yet. Not for a long time.

Pushing all thoughts of marriage out of his mind, he tried to extricate himself from the tiny woman next to him, but she gripped him tight and, in a half whisper, said, "Stay with me. Please?"

He was surprised that she had awoken. "Are you certain?"

"Yes," she said in a small voice, as though embarrassed to admit she needed him.

Needing no persuasion, he slipped beneath the covers and turning her gently around, drew her against his muscular torso so they were spooning. His big arms encompassed her and, within minutes, he could hear her even, steady breathing. For him, the task was not so easy. Her closeness did absolutely nothing to dampen his desire.

Sophia awoke feeling very refreshed. Her eyes fluttered open and she stared out of the big lattice windows, for a few moments feeling very comfortable and relaxed. It was then that she became aware of the large arm that lay across her waist and the hard body behind her. Memories of last night flooded back and she gulped when she remembered asking him to stay with her. God's Bones. Did that make her a wanton? She almost groaned aloud.

She then realised that during the night, her shift had ridden up and she could feel her bare bottom pressing against something hard. Her eyes grew wide with shock when she had an idea of what it was.

For a moment, she froze, wondering how to move without waking him up, and then she shifted slightly in preparation, but his arm immediately tightened around her. She froze again and then nearly jumped out of her skin when he moved his mouth close to her ear and said, "Good morning, Sophia."

He moved his mouth and kissed her jawline, making a steady path of kisses down to her shoulder. Sophia could hardly concentrate. The feeling was divine. The knowledge that she was doing something wicked and naughty seemed to fuel her desire. She felt his hand move from her waist to her raised shift, caressing a steady path to her bosom. She made no move to stop him. It was too heavenly and she was too aroused.

He cupped her breast and his fingers teased the nipple all

the while his mouth grazed her shoulder with searing kisses. She could feel his manhood pushing against her bottom and, inquisitive, she pushed against him. She heard his sharp intake of breath and then his hand moved down over her belly, down farther still, to her Venus mons, and then slipped between the folds of her womanhood. Her thighs parted naturally, seeking to experience this newfound sensation.

***

Jack easily found her small nub of desire and began a circular motion that soon had Sophia panting with desire, seeking release.

His cock was harder than rock and he would have liked nothing more than to sink into her warm sheath, but he would not take her virginity and ruin her. He only wanted to give her pleasure. Hearing her small cries, gave him satisfaction, and at the moment, it was all he could ask for. She was nearing her pinnacle, her muscles tightening, her cries increasing. A few moments later, her whole body first stiffened and then shuddered as she attained her climax, her head falling back with abandon.

Then, without further preamble, he turned her around and kissed her, parting her lips with his tongue to plunder her depths. She opened up for him, her arms entwining behind his neck, her soft body almost driving him insane. He was so close to giving in to his desires that it took all his effort and strength to deny himself the pleasure.

Finally, pulling away, he stared into her heavy-lidded, soft-green eyes. She looked even more beautiful than usual. He wondered if she would feel anger towards him for his actions, but in their shimmering depths, he saw only a soft awakening.

In that moment, he knew he was falling for her.

Sophia had never felt such pleasure, and even though she knew it was something an unmarried woman shouldn't do, she cared not. At that moment, she felt no shame. She stared into Jack's handsome face and realised she was falling in love with him. But she also understood that their relationship could never come to anything. He was a pirate. What life would that mean for her? But for now, she was content to enjoy his company on his ship. She would meet up with her brother in two months or so and start her new life with him and their new home.

And she would most probably never encounter Jack again. The thought made her immediately sad and she thrust the notion aside. Raising her hand, she cupped Jack's face and smiled. "Kiss me again, Jack."

He grinned and, lowering his head, captured her lips once again. Sophia lost herself to his masterful kiss, concentrating only on the here and now. The future could wait.

For the next week, Jack kept to his sofa at night, not trusting himself not to give in to his overwhelming desire for Sophia. She was inexperienced and it would be easy to take advantage of her innocence. That wouldn't sit well with him. He would never forgive himself.

They would reach Bordeaux tomorrow where they would fill up with fresh supplies of food and water. It was a lively port and he was looking forward to showing Sophia around. If she was good, he would treat her to a meal, maybe even buy her a gift.

His thoughts were interrupted by Grimes calling down from the crow's nest, "Sail ho, Cap'n."

He immediately reached into his jacket and pulled out his spyglass. Raising it to his right eye, he focussed on the horizon. Sure enough, there was a ship and she seemed to be heading straight in their direction.

"Does she fly a flag?" he called up to Grimes.

"No, Cap'n. None that I can see."

His brow furrowed. Was she friend or foe? Only time would tell. Calling out to John, the quartermaster, he told him to prepare for the worst. Soon, John was bellowing orders to the crew and the deck came alive with movement.

Jack remained vigilant as the ship drew ever nearer, and then raising his spyglass again, his face broke out in a huge smile. It was *The Blooming Belle*, a ship he recognised and a captain he had encountered on many an occasion. Bess Adams, a fiery, dark-haired vixen whom he had tried taming and failed miserably. But it had been fun while it lasted. She was far too wild and would never submit to any man, but she made a great captain.

He lowered the spyglass and waited for her to come alongside.

After finishing her current book, Sophia left the cabin and wandered up onto the main deck to get some fresh air. Her eyes widened when she saw that there was a big ship floating right next to *Blythe Spirit*, something she hadn't expected to see.

Suddenly, she heard a hearty laugh and recognised it was coming from Jack. She looked across to the other ship, to find him leaning against a tall mast, completely at ease and in conversation with a dark-haired woman. To her shock, she was wearing britches, just like a man. But her curves were obvious, and even from this distance, Sophia could see she was beautiful. Her long black hair, tied at the nape of her neck, curled almost to her bottom.

Sophia walked nearer to the railing so she could study them together. She seemed very familiar with Jack and her soft laughter drifted across on the wind, reaching Sophia's alert ears. Her eyes narrowed. Who was she?

The woman laughed again and laid her hand on Jack's sleeve. He made no move to remove it. Sophia felt like leaping across the dividing waters and removing it herself and then immediately admonished herself. What did it matter to her if they were familiar? She had no claim on Jack and he had none on her. She was being ridiculous.

But the green-eyed monster of jealousy continued to raise fire in her veins.

She knew she was being unreasonable, and with a whirl of her skirts, she ran back to the cabin, slamming the door behind herself. What she couldn't see, she couldn't fret about.

But that wasn't the case. She poured herself a goblet of red wine and sat at Jack's desk, brooding.

Jack's good mood quickly disappeared upon returning to his cabin and seeing Sophia's face. There was barely concealed fury lurking beneath her mask of complacency. He could see it in her eyes. The green emeralds sparked with fire.

"What's that look on your face for, Sophia?" he asked her.

She raised her chin a little. "It's nothing."

He shook his head. "I know when something is wrong. You cannot hide it from me. So, tell me."

"I told you, it's nothing."

"If you don't tell me, I'll spank you until you do. Your choice," he warned her.

"Fie, that's your answer to everything. If I choose not to tell you, that's my decision."

He gave her a hard look and realized that the only way to get her to tell him her problem was a sound spanking. She was far too stubborn for her own good.

Striding over, he grabbed her upper arm and quickly upended her over his lap as he sat down on the edge of the bed. Throwing her skirts over her back and parting her bloomers, he immediately started peppering her bottom with short, sharp smacks.

"If you have a problem, you talk about it. You don't bottle it up and hope it's going to go away. It's not good for your well-being."

Her small, indignant voice rose up from behind her curtain of hair. "And you think you're concerned about my well-being… ouch!"

He gave her several more sharp spanks that had her squirming to get away, but he held her fast. She was no match for his masculine strength.

"I'm very concerned with your well-being, Sophia. After all, I share a cabin with you, and if you're in high dudgeon, it affects me." He gave her several more spanks and was happy to see her bottom had turned a pretty shade of pink.

He finally let her up, and before she could move away from him, he sat her down on his lap. "Now, tell me what is bothering you."

Sophia winced when her tender bottom made contact with his thigh and would have sprung up again if Jack hadn't had such a strong hold on her.

She sullenly looked into his eyes and knew he wasn't

going to release her until she revealed to him why she was so angry.

He quirked an eyebrow. "Do you wish me to continue?"

Sophia rolled her eyes and then, looking down at the floor, she huffed, "I didn't like seeing you with that... that... woman."

She had wanted to call her something else, but common sense told her not to. It was bad enough having to reveal her feelings without throwing insults at someone she didn't even know.

For a moment, there was silence. Sophia raised her eyes to his and was surprised to see him smiling.

"Why are you smiling like that?" she asked him, irked.

"Well, I believe you might be jealous right now, which makes me happy."

"Hmph, why would I be jealous? Don't get the wrong idea."

His eyes crinkled with mirth and he dipped his head to capture her lips. She tried to resist at first, but he was insistent, and soon, she succumbed to his charms, opening her lips to receive his demanding kiss.

He kissed her thoroughly, and when he had finished, he pulled away and looked into her eyes, his expression fierce. "As long as I'm with you, I need no one else, sweet Sophia. There is no need for jealousy."

Sophia lay her head against his chest, knowing he truly meant those words. She could feel the beating of his heart beneath the fabric of his shirt.

"I feel foolish," she admitted.

"Don't be. It's only natural. After all, I'm so handsome that I literally have to stop women falling at my feet."

Sophia raised her eyes to his, and seeing the humour within, she playfully smacked him on the shoulder. "Fie, you're too arrogant for words!"

"Come, kiss me, and help me repent."

Sophia giggled and then placed her lips against his, whispering, "I don't know if I can, but I don't mind trying."

All thoughts of jealousy were forgotten as Jack skillfully claimed Sophia's lips for his own.

Chapter 7

PORT OF BORDEAUX...

Jack stood on the foredeck next to John as *Blythe Spirit* maneuvered into the port of Bordeaux. The sun shone down from a clear blue sky and he could already feel they were going to be in for a very hot spell. The sort of weather that would be great for a swim. He knew of a wonderful tranquil spot along the river that had its own little beach. He'd swum there many times with the crew and it was a great way of having a thorough wash—something that was always hard to do when on board ship. His thoughts turned to Sophia and he wondered if she knew how to swim. It was surprising how many people didn't. But either way, it would cool her down. He imagined her slender form revealed by wet clinging clothes and smiled wickedly. Yes, taking her bathing was a splendid idea.

The crew quickly set about securing the ship as she docked, throwing ropes to the mooring men and John bellowing out orders in his loud, commanding voice. Leaving them to finalise the procedure, Jack retreated to his cabin, to prepare to disembark.

Sophia was seated on the edge of the bed, already pulling on her boots. Her hair was neatly plaited and she was dressed in one of the two dresses she had brought with her.

"That reminds me," Jack remarked, looking her up and down, "I must buy you some more dresses today. You'll need some for England and something lighter for today. The sun is already fierce. Maybe a parasol as well."

"And a fan," Sophia added, smiling. "I can tap you with it when you do something wrong," she concluded with a wicked chuckle.

Jack immediately walked over to her and, grabbing her arm, pulled her straight against his chest. His eyes peered into hers. "You think to strike me, madam?"

She laughed up at him. "As if I would do such a thing."

"Hmm. Yes, I think you damned well would. But I have a remedy for that." He ran his hand over her delectable bottom and squeezed her flesh. He heard her sharp intake of breath and his loins immediately stirred. Lowering his lips, he claimed hers in a passionate kiss. She responded fervently, running her hands up over his chest to entwine at the nape of his neck, submitting herself to his exploring tongue.

A little while later, they broke apart, breathless.

"I think we should venture into town sooner, rather than later, before I do something we'll both regret."

"What do you mean?" she asked, her innocent eyes staring up at him.

"Sophia, you'll be my undoing. Come, follow me."

He strode to the door with her close behind. She was far too tempting and didn't even realise it. If he didn't leave now, he could end up giving in to his desires, and then where would he be?

Several hours later, they returned to the ship, Jack weighed down by several bags and his coffers much lighter. But it was worth it. They had dined at one of the small inns along the river and then ventured into one of the clothing boutiques, where Sophia had delighted in everything. She now had several dresses in both heavy and light fabrics, a fan, bloomers, two shifts and even a swimming dress. The boutique thankfully had a large selection of ready-made dresses to choose from, as they would only be in port a few days and had no time for a custom-made wardrobe.

One thing he had found out was that Sophia could swim, her brother having taught her years ago. He was glad for it because their trip to the secluded beach would be even more enjoyable.

Walking up the gangplank, he was greeted by several of the crew who openly laughed at the sight of him carrying Sophia's bags.

Upon seeing their captain's look turn fierce, they quickly stopped. Jack planted his feet on the deck and said aloud, "If I hear so much as a titter from any of you, all rum rations will be withdrawn until tomorrow." He stood firmly, glaring at them until the crew shook their heads glumly and muttered amongst themselves.

They failed to see Jack's wink that he gave Sophia before he turned and walked down the two steps to his quarters. It was always best to keep the crew on their toes. The captain's command was everything, and if you lost it, then a mutiny could follow. And that wasn't going to happen on Jack's watch!

The next morning...

Sophia stood at the ship's railings and watched the quayside with interest. It was quite busy, and standing in the shade of one of the tall masts, she looked at the people walking past.

Jack had gone into town with John, to trade his cargo—most of which was her brother's. But he had given her some good news in the fact that he had decided to share the proceeds with her and Isaac. Half for his crew and half for them. On the proviso that she would ensure Isaac never sought any revenge against him. She had readily agreed; it seemed more than fair.

She pulled a face, remembering why she was on the ship in the first place—to join up with her brother. But there was nothing she could do about it now. To be honest, she was enjoying her time on board. It made a wonderful change from being at home and having to put up with her father and his moods.

She wiped her brow. It was far too hot to stay in the cabin so she had decided to come up on deck to try to get some relief, but the wind was absent. Jack had promised they would be going for a swim later. She was so looking forward to it. She looked down at the waterline and imagined dipping herself in the cool river. It was beyond appealing.

She looked up again to see if she could spy Jack coming back, but there was no sign of him as yet. She was starting to get impatient.

Suddenly, she felt a presence next to her and looked up. It was Hawkins, the first mate.

"Excuse me, miss. I wondered if ye could give me some advice."

Sophia raised an eyebrow. "Of course."

"There's a girl I 'ave a fancy for and I was wondrin' like, if ye could… well, if ye could write me a letter to give to 'er."

"Oh. I see." She quickly realised he couldn't write. "Well, I don't see why not." It couldn't do any harm as far as she could see. She told him she would be right back and quickly went to the cabin to seek out some paper, ink and a dip pen. Besides, she loved a good romance story and this was a real life one.

She returned with the materials and settled herself down on one of the steps leading up to the foredeck. "So, who is she?"

Hawkins looked sheepish. "She's a merchant's daughter called Natalie. Right pretty, she is."

"Is she French?"

"Aye, but she can speak a bit o' English. Enough to understand me anyways."

He was clearly smitten and Sophia grinned. Placing the pen in the ink, she asked him what he wanted to say and began to copy it down onto the paper for him. Blowing the paper to dry the ink, she rolled it into a scroll and handed it to him. "Good luck."

"Thank ye, miss. Much appreciated."

She watched him run down the gangplank with a spring in his step, and smiling happily, she returned to the cabin to replace Jack's writing instruments. She hoped Natalie would appreciate Hawkins. He was about Sophia's age and was quite a good looking fellow. But time would tell.

Later that afternoon, Jack took her to the secluded beach as he had promised her. It was beautiful, not a soul around. It had taken a good half an hour's walk along a winding path through the forest, but he had told her it would be worth it. And indeed, he was right.

She had put her swimming dress beneath her day dress, and with a little bit of effort, she shrugged out of the attire and stepped towards the water line.

As the cool water touched her ankles and then her thighs, Sophia gasped at the drop in temperature. Her body was so hot, even more so after the walk, that the water felt almost too cold but she carried on walking until she was up to her waist.

She laughed and turned around to tell Jack how gorgeous it was, but the words died in her mouth when she saw him.

Stripped down to his britches, Sophia could see his whole torso. Broad shoulders led down to a bronzed, hardened torso with strong, muscular arms. He was truly magnificent.

Sophia quickly turned back and stared across the river, hoping her blushes would lessen. Dipping lower in the water, she continued until most of her body was submerged. Gently, she patted some of the fresh water on her face to cool her hot cheeks and then began to swim.

"I told you it would be refreshing, didn't I?" Jack said, reaching her side.

"It's blissful," she agreed. "It's so unbearably hot today. I'm glad we came."

"I thought you'd appreciate it. We'll stay for a while, there's no hurry. We can dry off on the beach before heading back."

Suddenly, she felt his hands spanning her waist. "Oh!" she gasped, but it was quickly stifled when his mouth covered hers. He pulled her against him and kissed her soundly before releasing her.

She looked up at him, her eyes wide. "Jack, what if someone sees us?"

"There's no one here. Besides, I don't care. Do you?" His eyes looked deep into hers and she giggled.

"No, I don't think I do!"

With a low laugh, he captured her lips once again. She had never been kissed so thoroughly or in such a situation.

The water lapped around them, doing nothing to cool their ardour.

Jack's hand crept lower and gently covered one of her buttocks, drawing her against his hard length and leaving her in no doubt as to his arousal.

Finally, they broke apart, both panting from desire.

"Come, let's have a swim. I need to cool down before I leave the water, or should I say *before* I am able to leave the water."

Sophia chuckled wickedly. "Well, fie, it's your own fault for kissing me."

"Is it now?" Jack's eyes darkened and Sophia, seeing his intent, squealed. But she was too late. Jack grabbed her and threw her up in the air so that when she came down, she went straight beneath the surface.

She came up sputtering within seconds and cursing him loudly. He laughed heartily and swam off. She tried chasing him, but she was no match for his strength.

After another ten minutes of larking around, they decided to leave the water and dry off. The heat of the sun had them dry in no time. Sophia's hair was still damp, but she re-braided it and it looked as neat as it had that morning. Laughing happily, and at ease in each other's company, they walked back to the ship.

The next morning, Legrand Warehouse...

Jack looked across the table at Henri Legrand. His colour was high with anger and he thrust a piece of paper towards Jack.

"Read that!"

"What is it?"

"Just read it."

Jack leaned over and took the paper, turning it around so he could read it. It was a love letter, and at the bottom, it was signed by Hawkins of *Blythe Spirit*. Hawkins? What the devil was he doing writing love letters? In fact, he couldn't even write as far as Jack knew. Something was afoot.

"Why is one of your crew writing to my daughter?" Legrand demanded.

Jack frowned. "How should I know? I'm not privy to their every movement." He could see the letter had obviously angered him and would have to watch his words carefully. He was so near to negotiating a good price for his goods that he didn't want to irk the man.

Legrand stood up and paced the floor. "Do you seriously think I'd want a man like him for a son-in-law? That I'd give up my precious daughter to a low life scurvy dog like that?"

Jack watched him warily. "You have nothing to worry about if your daughter has no feelings for him."

He stopped pacing and banged his fist down on the table. "Silly girl thinks she loves him."

"Oh, I see," Jack said.

He pointed his finger in Jack's face. "Your crew should mind their own business. Tell him from me, that if I see him anywhere near my daughter, he won't live to tell the tale."

Jack rubbed his brow. He wanted to tell Legrand to go and jump off a cliff but he was a good merchant. One Jack used often. He had no desire to hamper any future business deals because of what might turn out to be just an infatuation. Standing up, he scraped the chair back and said, "Very well. You have my word that I'll tell him." He didn't add that Hawkins might not listen to him. It all depended on how deep his infatuation with the girl went.

John was waiting for him outside, puffing away with satisfaction on his clay pipe. He immediately noted Jack's frown. "Something up, Cap'n?"

"You could say that. It seems Hawkins has a passion for Legrand's daughter."

"Has he, by God. Blow me down." He laughed and then added, "And I take it, Legrand's not so keen?"

Jack shook his head. "You could say that."

"Do you want me to say something to Hawkins?"

"If you would. It might be better coming from you. Poor sod. Tell him to find another lass to bestow his charms on, preferably one in Portsmouth."

John blew out a big line of smoke and, shaking his head, remarked, "Why he had to choose a Frenchie, I've no idea."

Arriving back at the ship, John went in search of Hawkins and Jack went to his quarters. Sophia looked up as he entered. She was sitting on the cushioned window seat, reading one of his books and looked very settled. He could honestly say it was a pleasure to come back to such a winsome looking woman.

"How did it go?" she asked him, closing her book.

"Quite well. We finalise the deal tomorrow when we deliver the goods. He's a peculiar fellow."

"Oh?"

Jack poured himself a glass of rum and held up the decanter. "Would you like some?"

Sophia shook her head, waiting for him to elaborate. "So, how is he peculiar? Does he have a large nose? A protruding forehead? What?"

Jack laughed. "No, nothing like that. He's just very serious. Very dour." He took a big draught of the rum before continuing. "And it would seem Hawkins has taken a liking to his daughter. Something that he has taken umbrage against."

He noted Sophia's eyes had widened slightly. "Is her name Natalie?" she asked.

Jack nodded. "How did you know that?" Then the penny dropped. "Did you write that letter for him?"

Her cheeks suffused with colour. "Well, yes, I did, but I had no idea who she was. He just asked me very nicely if I'd write him a letter."

"And would you jump off the side of the ship if he asked you?"

"Of course not. Don't be silly!" Sophia snapped. "If you must scold me, tell me what I did wrong."

Jack tapped his fingers on the desk. "It's not your place to write letters on behalf of my crew. I know your intentions were good, but you'll not do so again." He fixed her with a look and she squirmed uncomfortably.

Walking over, he drew her into his arms and said, "I would have your promise that you won't do it again. If you do, you'll know the consequences."

A thrill shot through Sophia. She couldn't help herself. When he spoke with such authority, it kindled a fire within her.

Placing one hand on his chest, she smiled up at him and promised not to do it again. Her other hand was behind her back with her fingers crossed. As far as she was concerned, he was overreacting. What possible harm could a little love letter do?

She opened her mouth when Jack's lips touched hers, and when they burned a steady path of fiery kisses down her neck, she arched her back in response, forgetting all about letters and what she should and shouldn't do, just concentrating on the here and now. It was heavenly.

The next morning...

Jack arose early to oversee the delivery of the goods to Legrand, so left to her own devices, Sophia wandered around on deck to get some fresh air. Thankfully, the day wasn't so hot because of the large white clouds intermittently blocking the sun's rays. It was a relief from the previous day's overwhelming heat.

She noticed Hawkins standing by the railing looking rather forlorn, and despite Jack's warning not to intervene, she wandered over to see how he was. That, surely, wasn't forbidden.

Hawkins looked at her and pulled a face. "That letter didn't work, miss."

"She never replied then?" Sophia queried.

He shook his head. "No. I think, even if she wanted to, 'er father would stop 'er."

"Does she love you?"

"Aye, she's said so. But I ain't ever gonna 'ave a chance if 'er father's always around," he lamented.

Sophia thought hard. He looked so sad that she wanted to help the two of them. She had thought of a plan last night but had put it to the back of her mind due to Jack's command that she shouldn't get involved. But how could she not?

"Maybe I can help you," Sophia offered.

"Are you trying to get me killed?" Hawkins exclaimed, shaking his head.

"Killed?" Sophia gasped. "Natalie's father has threatened to kill you?"

"No, but John has," he said forlornly.

"Oh, fie, he is just bluffing. Take no notice. Now, what if I have an idea?" Her eyes sparkled with mischief.

Hawkins grinned and, riled up by her enthusiasm, asked, "What do you suggest?"

Sophia left the ship and, walking fast, hurried along the quayside. She knew what she was doing was risky, but she felt compelled to do so. Hawkins was depending on her.

She wore a scarf draped over her head which she held together with one hand under her chin, the rolled up love letter in her other hand.

Hawkins had told her where Natalie would be. She served customers in a small shop next to her father's big warehouse. That was how they'd met in the first place, when Hawkins had bought a brooch for his mother.

Sophia knew all too well what a controlling father was like and her heart went out to Natalie. If she truly did have feelings for Hawkins, then maybe it would be better for her to leave home and start a new life with him in England.

So, with a determined stride, she searched out the shop. She knew Jack would be nearby, hence the disguise. But Hawkins had assured her that he would be in the warehouse around the other side.

The shop came into view and Sophia eyed it cautiously, looking left and right for any sign of anyone else in the vicinity. Deciding it was all clear, she stepped up to the door and opened it.

A pretty, dark-haired girl greeted her, and with big eyes, Sophia approached her.

"Good morning, are you Natalie?" Sophia asked.

The girl nodded.

Making sure the coast was clear, Sophia lowered her scarf and handed her the rolled up letter. "This is from Hawkins."

The girl's face lit up with surprise. "Oh, *mon dieu*, he has sent me another letter. I thought my father had warned him off."

"Hawkins is made of sterner stuff than that." Sophia grinned. "I can take a reply if you like. Is there somewhere I can wait?"

"Oh, that's so nice of you."

Suddenly, the door opened behind her. Natalie's mouth dropped open and she looked over Sophia's shoulder in shock. Sophia whirled around to find an older man staring at her, and by the stern look on his face, it could only be one man. Natalie's father.

Quickly, Sophia turned back with the intent of snatching up the letter before he had time to see it, but in one stride, he was on her and ripped it out of her hands.

Realising she was in trouble, Sophia sought to escape, but Legrand's hand snaked out and held her upper arm fast. "And just where might you be going in such a hurry? Looks to me like you have something to hide, miss."

With his other hand, he rolled out the paper and quickly read it, muttering an oath when he realised what it was.

"Why, you little…"

Sophia stared at him in fright. He was so angry. Struggling, she tried to get away. "Let me go, sir!"

He gave her a hard stare, his eyes blazing. "I should have you flogged."

"Papa!" Natalie cried.

Sophia's eyes nearly popped out of her head. "W-what for?"

"Having a hand in this." Suddenly, he released her. "Who are you?"

"Just a friend," she whispered.

"A friend? What, of this varmint?" He shook the letter in her face and she winced. "So you're off the same ship?"

Sophia nodded.

He gave her a hard stare. Sophia regarded him silently, her heart in her mouth, wondering what he was going to do.

The door was only a few footsteps away and she moved one foot nearer to it, ready to dart out in a heartbeat if he decided to carry out his threat.

But luck was on her side, for his temper seemed to diminish somewhat. "I guess you're only the messenger. My anger should be directed at this low life varmint. I suggest you leave this minute before I change my mind."

Sophia didn't need telling twice. With her tail between her legs, she ran as fast as she could for the safety of the ship.

Chapter 8

JACK LOOKED with satisfaction at the large crates and sacks stacked up in a corner of Legrand's warehouse. He had made a tidy penny out of their plunder; the crew would be having a good drink tonight, that was certain.

He looked up when he saw Legrand enter the main door at the other end of the warehouse, ready to welcome him, but his smile died when he saw his face. He looked angry.

John, standing next to him, noted it as well. "Someone isn't happy."

Jack sighed inwardly and muttered under his breath, "What the devil's wrong now?"

Legrand wasted no time in voicing his anger. "I told you to keep that bastard away from my daughter, yet you've failed to do so!" He thrust the rolled parchment at him. "He's even bolder than before. What sort of captain cannot control his crew?"

Jack felt the anger rise in him like a tide. Who did Legrand think he was talking to? Trying to remain calm, he unrolled the letter and read the contents.

Before he had a chance to digest the words, Legrand said

angrily, "He's lucky I didn't catch him in the act. He got a slip of a girl to deliver the note instead."

Jack frowned, a troublesome thought entering his mind. "A girl?"

"Yes, pretty little blonde. Said she was off your ship. Who is she?"

Jack groaned inwardly. Sophia. Even after she had promised him not to interfere, she had gone ahead and done it anyway. Oh boy, was she in trouble.

"She's my ward."

Legrand raised an eyebrow. "So, you cannot control your crew or your ward?"

"That ain't no way to speak to the captain," John growled. Legrand ignored him.

Jack's jaw tightened. "You have my word, both will be punished."

"I should hope so. It's your responsibility. If you want to do business in the future, then I would have your assurance that your crew stay away from my daughter. It's as simple as that."

Jack's control of his temper began to wane. "Don't threaten me. I've given my word they'll be punished and that'll be an end to it."

"You gave me your word last time. Yet still, Hawkins persists. The man is a pest."

Jack muttered an oath, and then turning to John, he decided to play Legrand at his own game. "John, reload the wares onto the cart."

For a moment, John looked a little nonplussed and then understood Jack's intention. "Aye, aye, Cap'n, sir."

Legrand's jaw dropped open and he quickly ran in front of John. "I mean to say, there's no need to be hasty! We needn't let this hinder our deal."

Just as Jack had thought. Legrand was all bluff and no substance.

"Very well, but never threaten me again. As I've told you already, I *will* see to it that both parties are reprimanded for their involvement," Jack promised him. "And that's an end to it."

He wanted to say so much but didn't want to jeopardize the sale of his merchandise. Calling his bluff was one thing, but the tables could turn in an instant and he would have to travel a lot farther to sell his cargo.

Besides, maybe Legrand was right. One thing was certain, both culprits would receive a punishment. He would leave Hawkins to John's wrath, but the little madam was most definitely his responsibility.

His speech seemed to satisfy Legrand for now. "Very well. Now, come to the house and we'll finalise the deal."

Much later, Jack and John walked back along the quay towards the ship, both carrying a fair-sized pouch full of coins.

"What do you want me to do about Hawkins, Cap'n?" John asked.

"Give him a punishment that will make him think twice before going anywhere near Legrand's daughter. Nothing too harsh, but something that he won't forget in a while."

"Aye, Cap'n."

They boarded the ship and Jack went straight to his quarters, where he intended to interrogate a certain wayward little madam.

Jack found Sophia sitting demurely on the sofa reading a book. He looked directly at her and asked, "How did you occupy your time whilst I was away this morning?"

He watched her fidget nervously, and placing her book down, she replied, "Nothing much. I had a quick walk on deck to get some fresh air and then I decided to read for a while."

He leaned against his desk and folded his arms, fixing her with a hard stare. "Really?"

He noted her cheeks beginning to flush and she licked her lips before replying. "Yes, really. What do you think I've been doing?"

"You've been off the ship."

"No, I haven't!"

"I know you have, but I want you to tell me why."

She stared at him and then looked away, lowering her lashes to hide her guilt.

"You're not going to tell me what happened, are you? Well, if you don't feel like telling me, should I have the quartermaster handle this? Should I have you keel hauled? Walk the plank?"

Her eyes shot to his. "You wouldn't dare do such a thing!"

"Wouldn't I?" He watched her carefully. He knew exactly what she'd done, but he'd give her time to confess. He was still going to spank her, but her confession all depended on how severe her punishment would be.

"I have no idea what you are talking about. I didn't leave the ship."

"Keep the story up and I will spank you longer and harder."

"Spank me?" she gasped.

"What did I tell you about writing letters for Hawkins? What did I specifically tell you not to do?" He stood up and began walking over to her. She shrank back in her seat, her eyes wide.

"I-I didn't write any more letters. Honest, I didn't. I've no idea what note you're speaking about."

"You mean this note." He withdrew the rolled up love letter from his waistcoat and then looked at her accusingly.

"But…"

He reached down and grabbed her arm, hauling her off the sofa and sitting down at the same time, quickly placing her face down over his lap.

"Jack! No! Please!" She tried to protest, but he held her fast.

Pulling up her dress and parting her bloomers, his hand descended straight onto her exposed bottom. He rained down several hard swats on her backside before saying anything. "You conniving little madam! You plotted all this behind my back."

Jack spanked her hard for a good few minutes, until Sophia was writhing in pain. It was unbearable! She begged him to stop, but her words fell on deaf ears.

He leaned down nearer to her ear. "Not yet—not until your bottom is burning uncomfortably. You lied to me and that's unforgiveable!"

His hand began a steady rhythm, alternating between cheeks, until her bottom felt like it was on fire. She tried throwing her hand around to rub it better but he just slapped it away.

"Please stop! It hurts!" she wailed.

"No! You deserve this, besides which, it's supposed to hurt! I'm going to make sure you don't sit comfortably for a few days so the next time you think of doing anything so foolish, you might remember not to!"

Sophia's face screwed up with pain when another slap hit her sit spots. He meant business. His large hand felt as though it was made of iron. Why, oh, why had she interfered and written that blasted letter? She had been spanked enough times by now to realise that Jack would punish her.

After several more very hard spanks, he finally stopped. He rested his hand on her bottom and rubbed in slow circles before gently pulling her up to sit on his knee. She sniffled and buried her face in his chest.

When her sniffles had subsided, he lifted her face to his, making her look at him. "Why would you go against my wishes, Sophia?"

She looked down, ashamed. "I just wanted two people in love to be happy."

"And you think I don't?" He shook his head. "It's not our place to intervene. Natalie's father was beside himself with rage. You're lucky he didn't take matters into his own hands."

Sophia's eyes widened remembering how angry Natalie's father was.

"Where was Hawkins? Did he escort you?" Jack asked her.

Somehow, she knew her answer wasn't going to be well-received but she didn't want to lie anymore and get herself into even more trouble, if that was possible. She shifted uneasily on his lap and her tender bottom zinged into life.

"He didn't come," she said in a small voice.

"Are you mad?" he asked incredulously. "You walked along the quayside in a foreign country all by yourself? It's God's mercy that you weren't accosted!"

"There was no danger that I could see," she told him defiantly.

"There are cutthroats around here aplenty. They could easily have plucked you from the quay in the blink of an eye. You were beyond foolish. In fact, I should punish you again for your actions." His eyes darkened with anger.

"No! I promise I've learned my lesson." she cried, but the truth of his words had frightened her. She had not considered any misadventures when she had set out to help Hawkins. She flushed nervously.

"Maybe you've been punished enough, but know this, my little rebel, you will not step off this ship without me by your side. Is that clear?"

Sophia nodded.

He dipped his head and slowly kissed her ripe mouth. "Did I hurt you?"

"You have a hard hand, Jack," she admitted, rubbing her injured posterior. "It stung."

"Good!" Jack told her. "Then the next time you're tempted to act rashly, you'll remember my hard hand and act more prudently, won't you, my love? " His eyes were twinkling as he spoke and Sophia couldn't help but smile at his handsome face. Despite the pain in her bottom, she knew she had fallen in love with the man in front of her.

Whether they had a future together, she knew not, but for now, she was content with experiencing the here and now. It would suffice.

Blythe Spirit weighed anchor that very afternoon and plotted a course for England. Jack was looking forward to seeing his family and regaling them with tales of the last few months. A good drink together was what he needed. He had plenty of Bordeaux wine on board, some taken as plunder, a lot recently purchased from Legrand.

Standing at the wheel, overseeing their departure, his thoughts turned to the winsome woman in his quarters. He would introduce her to his brother Logan's wife, Sapphire. She had been just as rebellious from the few snippets Logan had revealed to him. Perhaps she would help tame the firebrand for him. He smiled. Although maybe he didn't want her tamed. Having to punish that naughty bottom of hers, was most definitely no chore.

They sailed on through virtually unoccupied seas the first day and the next day as well. Rounding Finisterre Point, other ships began to appear until, finally, on the fifth morning, they approached West Bay in Bridport.

Sophia stood at the rail and looked at the grey mist swirling about the port. It didn't look very inviting. Jack joined her and immediately noted her expression.

"Don't worry, it isn't always so grim." He chuckled. "Despite its reputation."

Sophia couldn't help but laugh. "I shall take your word for that."

Half an hour later, the ship was settled into its mooring and Jack asked Callum to go and hire a carriage for him and Sophia. He would leave the ship in John's trusted hands whilst visiting his brother.

They traveled the twenty miles separating West Bay Port and Arlington House, arriving by midday. As their carriage drew to a stop, the two grooms jumped down from their outside seat behind the coach and hurried to open the door and lower the step, allowing the passengers to descend. Wellham, Logan's steward, hurried from the house to welcome them and take their luggage.

Sophia looked up at the large house in awe. It was magnificent. Jack took her elbow and directed her towards the stone steps that led up to the entrance. She couldn't help feeling a little nervous about meeting Jack's brother and sister-in-law.

No sooner than they stepped inside, a woman's voice could be heard. "Molly! Don't touch that!"

A little giggle could be heard and then a tiny little girl appeared, waving a spoon in the air and grinning from ear to ear. Sophia's eyes lit up at the sight of her. The girl came to an abrupt halt when she saw the strange people standing in the hallway and her eyes widened.

A young woman quickly appeared and swept the little girl up in her arms. "One of these days, Molly!" She suddenly realised there were people in the hall and she smiled prettily. "Jack!"

"Sapphire, you look gorgeous as ever." He walked over and, taking her hand, raised it to his lips and placed a kiss on the soft skin. She blushed.

Suddenly, a deep voice called down the stairs, "Enough of that!"

Jack glanced up and grinned. "Logan!"

A tall man descended the stairs. He was as handsome as Jack except his hair was a little darker, whereas Jack's had sun-kissed streaks. He clapped Jack on the back. "Good to see you, brother." His eyes fell on Sophia with interest and he looked at Jack. "Aren't you going to introduce us?"

"Of course. This is Sophia Thorn, of Thorn Creek Tobacco Plantation in Williamsburg."

Sophia inclined her head. "Nice to meet you, sir."

"Welcome to Arlington," he said with a warm smile. "Please, call me Logan. This is my wife, Sapphire, and our daughter, Molly."

Sophia smiled at Sapphire who grinned in return and said, "Come into the parlour and I will order some refreshments. You must be a little fatigued from the journey. Then you can tell me all about yourself."

Molly was staring at her with big blue eyes. She was a mirror image of her mother, with blonde ringlets framing her little face.

"Your daughter is delightful," Sophia said, gently tapping Molly on the nose. The little girl giggled in response.

"She has grown so much since I last saw her," Jack commented, following them into the parlour. His brother had been married for nigh on two and a half years and seemed blissfully happy. Sapphire was still quite feisty, but his brother knew exactly how to handle her.

A young maid appeared and took Molly away for her afternoon nap, leaving Sapphire time to entertain her guests. She ordered some refreshments, and leaving Jack to speak with Logan, she drew Sophia over to the other side of the room.

"So, I'm dying to know, what's your connection to Jack? Are you going to marry him?" Her eyes sparkled with interest.

Sophia's jaw dropped. "Oh, um, no."

"Oh? So how do you know him?"

"Well, it's a long story really."

"I have time." Sapphire grinned.

Sophia warmed to her and knew Sapphire wouldn't give up until she knew the truth. Taking a deep breath, she said, "Well, in a nutshell, I stowed away on his ship to get away from my father. Then we encountered my brother's ship, which had attacked Jack's ship before, so Jack took revenge and held me captive."

"What!" Sapphire exclaimed.

Sophia nodded.

"So if you're being held against your will, why don't you seek to escape?"

"Jack has promised my brother he'll return me to Jamestown, unharmed, in September."

"Oh, indeed, he would never hurt you!" Sapphire said, her eyes widening.

"I know that now." Although her bottom could testify against that. "And to be truthful, I'm enjoying the journey. My father is a tyrant and I'm glad to be away from him. That's why I ran away in the first place."

"Only to be taken hostage." Sapphire chuckled. "God's

bones. What a pickle you've found yourself in. You sound a little like me. Always finding yourself in trouble."

Sophia giggled.

"You and I shall be firm friends, I just know it," Sapphire stated. "It's a shame the weather is so dismal today," she lamented, looking out the window. "I should've liked to show you the grounds. Maybe tomorrow. We can have a more thorough chat when you're rested. Also, the men won't be there to listen, so you can tell me more intimate details." She chuckled wickedly.

Jack looked over at the two blonde beauties and said to Logan, "Why do I feel they're going to be trouble together?"

"If Sophia is anything like Sapphire, then you'll need your wits about you, brother." He sat back in his chair and studied Jack. "I still cannot believe you took her as a hostage against her brother."

"Bastard would've attacked the ship again if I hadn't. Anyway, he'll get her back again in a month or so."

Logan eyed him carefully. "Do you mean to give her back?"

"Of course. She's been nothing but a pain in my side since I found her." He smiled and Logan nodded knowingly.

"She's got under your skin, hasn't she?"

"No!" Jack said, affronted. "No woman will ever do that. I'll admit that I find her attractive. What man wouldn't? But she's also a spoiled brat and I've had to reprimand her on more than one occasion. What man would want such a woman for a wife?"

Logan laughed loudly and slapped his thigh. "I think I may have said the very same thing. Watch yourself. Before you know it, you won't be able to picture life without her."

Jack looked across the room to the wayward little rebel and had a feeling it was already too late, for the very idea of handing her back to her brother made bile rise in his throat. He had grown used to having her by his side. How was he going to cope when she had to leave him?

Chapter 9

THE NEXT DAY dawned bright and sunny. Sophia had slept deeply and awoke feeling rested and refreshed. She was certainly ready to have a wander around Arlington's grounds as Sapphire had mentioned to her.

She thought of Sapphire and smiled to herself. They were like peas in a pod; they could be sisters. She had warmed to her immediately.

Walking over to the bedroom window, she looked out onto the neat lawns. It was very pretty and well-maintained. She looked farther across and could see several horses in the pasture beyond the lawns. Her eyes lit up. Maybe she could go riding with Sapphire?

Suddenly, movement caught her eye and Jack and Logan came into view. They were walking along the drive, deep in conversation, Logan pointing into the distance at something.

They were both so handsome and cut such fine figures. She couldn't help but admire the brothers, her eyes focussing on Jack in particular. What would it be like to be married to such a man? She raised a hand to her lips, remembering their last kiss. Heat stole over her cheeks and she bit her bottom lip when a rush of desire swept through her.

As if on cue, Jack turned his head and looked up at her. She blushed even more deeply. Did he have a sixth sense? She lowered her hand and sent him a quick smile before turning and heading down to the dining room to break her fast, hoping the colour in her cheeks might subside on the way down!

Sapphire was already seated and beamed at her when she opened the door. "Good morning, Sophia. Come, take a seat and help yourself to some food. Hannah has made some lovely scrambled eggs and toast, or there is jam if you prefer."

Sophia slid into a seat opposite her. "Oh, this looks delicious." She pointed at a pot. "Is that coffee?"

Sapphire shook her head. "Tea. But I can order some coffee if you prefer."

"No, tea will be just fine."

Sapphire poured her a cup and pushed it forward. "Did you sleep well?"

"Like a log. I was so tired. Can we still look around the grounds today as you suggested? I saw some horses from the bedroom window. I would love to go and see them."

"Of course, we can. Beatrice will look after Molly for me. Do you ride?"

"I have done but not for a while. Do you?"

"Often. If you like, we can have a walk this morning and then go for a ride this afternoon." She turned and glanced up at the sky through the window. "It promises to be a beautiful day."

The door opened and Jack and Logan appeared.

"Good morning, ladies," Logan said, taking a seat. "I've just been showing Jack the new summer house."

"What do you think, Jack?" Sapphire asked him. "Do you like it?"

"It's a great addition to the house. I can see many moments spent there during those lovely hot evenings."

Sophia felt a tinge of envy. It all sounded so delightful. She would love to have been part of that, but her life wasn't here, it was in Williamsburg. Maybe one day that would change, but she would have to wait and see.

The men helped themselves to the array of food on the table and Sapphire poured them both a cup of tea.

"We're going into town tonight to meet with Father and Oliver," Logan informed his wife whilst buttering his toast.

"Can we come?" Sapphire asked.

Logan shook his head. "Not tonight. We have business to discuss and you'll only get bored."

"What if we promise not to interfere? I should like to go into town."

"Not tonight."

"But, Logan—"

"Sapphire. I said no." He fixed her with a look and Sapphire immediately pouted. Sophia looked from one to the other, wondering if an argument would ensue but it seemed Logan's word was law, for Sapphire refrained from any further objections.

After a few moments, she turned to Sophia and said, "Are you ready to see the grounds?"

Sophia nodded, and leaving the men to finish their breakfast, they put on their walking boots and left the house.

As they began their walk, Sophia sniffed the fresh country air appreciatively. "Ahh, how good that smells," she said. "It seems I've been at sea so long that I'd almost forgotten what good country air is like."

"It's beautiful here, isn't it?"

Halfway down to the pasture, Sapphire looked over her

shoulder to make sure they were alone and said, "You and I will come to the summer house this evening and have some of that lovely Bordeaux wine that Jack brought back." She gave a wicked chuckle. "Just because we cannot go into town, does not mean we cannot imbibe a few drinks, does it?"

Sophia laughed. "It sounds like fun to me. Will Logan object?"

"He won't know." Sapphire grinned.

"What if you get tipsy?"

"Ah, we'll be in bed long before they return. I doubt they'll be back before midnight. Their business meetings, as he calls them, are just a chance for the brothers to get together and drink themselves silly. So what's good for the goose is also good for the gander!" She looked at Sophia with a wicked smile and said, "Race you!" And picking up her skirts, she immediately broke into a run.

"Wait! That's not fair!" Sophia called out and immediately set about following after her. She caught up to her just as she reached the fence.

Holding her side from the exertion, Sophia panted. "That was totally unfair!"

"Ah, you're just annoyed you didn't win." She looked at her, her whole face alight with mischief. Sophia couldn't help but laugh.

"You must be such a handful for Logan."

"That's why he loves me." She grinned. "Talking of love, are you sure you don't have feelings for Jack? I've seen the looks you exchange and I'm certain he is attracted to you."

"Do you truly think so?"

Sapphire nodded emphatically. "Oh, yes."

"But that doesn't exactly mean he wants to marry me. I think I'm a thorn in his side. Thorn by name, thorn by nature." She giggled. "He's already spanked me several times for misbehaving."

"You, too?"

Sophia's eyes shot to Sapphire's. "Does your husband spank you?"

Sapphire nodded. "Lots."

"Lord, we are a pair, aren't we?"

Sapphire began to tell Sophia about Logan, confirming what Jack had told her already, that he used to captain *Blythe Spirit* before Jack. Piracy ran in the family and so did spanking their women, apparently. By the end of her story, Sophia felt even closer to Sapphire. It was quite a revelation.

One of the horses came up to be petted and Sapphire lifted her hand to caress the chestnut beauty. "This is Rosie. She's very docile. And see that one over there, that's Bess. She'll be perfect for you to ride this afternoon if you're still up to it?"

"Oh, I'd love to have a ride."

"Well, that's definite then. After luncheon, we'll take a ride across the fields. We can tell Stuart at the stables on our way back."

They walked back together, chatting amiably. Sophia felt she had found a true friend and it was a nice feeling.

That evening, Sapphire sat down on the plush sofa in the parlour opposite Sophia and listened to the front door close. Then, smiling conspiratorially, the pair rushed over to the window and concealing themselves behind the wooden shutters, they peered out and watched the men leave on their horses.

"How long shall we wait before heading off?" Sophia asked, peeking out carefully.

"Ten minutes or so should do it."

"I cannot believe you said we'd be doing embroidery! I've never embroidered in my life," Sophia commented.

"Ah, it's easy. I don't do it often, but it sounded good."

Ten minutes later, found the girls heading down to the summer house, a bottle of Bordeaux and two glasses in their hands.

The summer house was beautiful. It had several large patio doors that opened up to let the summer breeze in and two large chaise lounges, a low table and in one corner, and a rocking horse for Molly when she would be old enough to use it.

"Oh, this is gorgeous, Sapphire."

"I love it." She plumped up a couple of cushions and patted the seat. "Take a seat and I'll pour you a glass of this lovely beverage!"

She pulled the cork stopper off the wine and sniffed the contents, her eyes closing when the heady aroma assailed her senses. "Oh, yes, this is a good one."

Pouring two glasses, she handed one to Sophia and raised her glass. "To our new found friendship."

Sophia raised her glass and then sipped the wine. It was rich and fruity. "This is lovely. I can feel the heat of the alcohol already."

Two glasses later, and they were both feeling quite merry. The sun was still quite high in the sky so Sapphire told her to follow her over to one of the barns.

Intrigued, Sophia followed. Once inside and making sure they were alone, Sapphire walked to a trunk in one corner and, opening it, pulled out a small sword. Sophia gasped. "Is that yours!"

"Yes, isn't it lovely?" She held the blade up so it caught the sun and the rays reflected off the shiny metal. "Logan had it especially made for me."

"Can I have a go?"

Sapphire looked at her sharply. "Have you ever handled a sword?"

Sophia grinned and nodded. "My brother taught me from a very young age. He wanted me to know how to protect myself. I'm quite adept at using one. Let me show you."

Sapphire handed her the sword and she did a few practice moves, swishing the blade through the air and thrusting forward.

"I'm impressed, Sophia. I think we should have a practice together." She turned and walked over to the trunk and, digging around, brought out two larger swords. "I only have the one small blade, so I think to be fair, we should use the two bigger ones."

Sophia walked over and took one of the swords off her. "I'm only used to larger ones anyway, but I'd love to have a small one like yours. It's lighter and easier to brandish. I think when I return home, I'll see about having my own made."

The thought of home made her frown. She couldn't imagine being at Thorn Creek Plantation now. Hopefully, Isaac would have made enough money in between times to get their own place, or at least she could rent a small house, away from her odious father. She shuddered even thinking about him.

Sapphire noted it immediately. "What's wrong, Sophia?"

"I just thought about my father. I truly don't want to ever return home."

"Then don't!" Sapphire said. "Stay here if need be. He sounds awful and you deserve so much better." She raised her sword, and placing her other hand on her hip, she took a fighting stance. "Come, parry swords with me and pretend I'm your father!"

Sophia stepped back and, raising her sword, smiled and said, "Very well. On guard, mon amie!"

They started straight away, neatly dancing around each other, their skirts swishing as they parried back and forth, the blades slicing through the air and then coming together in a flash of steel.

It was exhilarating and Sophia loved it. She hadn't practised for ages, but she had forgotten nothing. Sapphire was really good and it seemed they were both equal in their expertise.

After a lot of cutting and thrusting, both girls' energy began to wane, not helped by their slightly tipsy condition. Sapphire suddenly took a step back and lowered her sword. "Fie, Sophia, you are accomplished!"

Sophia bowed eloquently. "My thanks, madam." And then she laughed loudly. "I haven't had this much fun in ages. We must do this again before I leave."

Placing their swords down, they both sat down on the dusty barn floor and leaned against the wooden slats, getting their breath back.

"Wait here. I'm going to fetch that other bottle of wine," Sapphire stated, getting to her feet. "I think we've earned it."

Sophia sat, quietly listening to the small birds chattering on the beams above as they flew in and out, the odd buzzing insect and the crickets chirping in the grass. It was a lovely time of year and she felt blessed that fate had ordained she experience such a perfect season for her first visit to England.

Sapphire returned with the two glasses and another bottle of Bordeaux. She poured them each a glass and sat down beside Sophia. Raising her glass, she clinked it with Sophia's and said, "To us!"

It wasn't long before they had polished off the bottle and Sophia's head was beginning to feel quite fuzzy.

"You know, *hic*, we should return to the house. I think I need to go to bed." She rubbed her brow.

"Oh, not yet!" Sapphire whined. "The sun will not set for another hour. We can have another sword fight. Come on." She stood up and swayed a little. "God's bones, that wine is strong."

Sophia closed one eye and peered at her. "I feel unusual."

Sapphire giggled. "Fie, Sophia, are you chickening out? Does that mean I'm the victor?"

"Ha! I'm no chicken! *Hic*, give me that sword." Sophia slowly got to her feet and steadied herself. "Lord, whose idea was this?"

Sapphire handed her a sword and brandished her own. "En guard!"

Sophia swore there were two of her, but bravely, she held up her sword and brandished it in the air. "Touché!"

Their swords touched and combat began, only this time, they kept missing each other. At one point, Sapphire fell to the floor and, giggling, quickly scrambled up again. "Oh my!"

Suddenly, a deep voice filled the air, stopping the pair of them in their tracks. They looked across to the barn door, their eyes wide with shock.

"What the devil do you think you're playing at?" It was Logan, and his anger was evident. Jack was right behind him, his face grim.

It would seem they had arrived back just in time. Jack looked down at the empty bottle of wine lying on its side and the two discarded glasses. They were clearly drunk, which might have been acceptable, except they were foolishly brandishing a sword at each other.

Logan stepped forward and took Sapphire by the arm, relieving her of the sword. "What were you thinking?" he admonished her.

"Logan, there is no need to be so angry. We were just having fun!" she complained, her bottom lip beginning to pout.

Sophia swayed slightly and blinked rapidly to clear her vision, gripping her sword tightly. A look of indignance settled on her face, and holding up her sword, she pointed it at Jack. "You cannot come here and spoil our fun!"

"Put the sword down, Sophia," Jack ordered her.

"No!"

Jack wasted no time, and stepping swiftly forward, he yanked the weapon from Sophia's hand. Then, jamming her beneath his arm, he smacked her posterior with several hard blows before forcing her back onto her feet before him, his hands gripping her shoulders hard. "Now, listen to me, you defiant little madam," he said in a hard, grim voice.

"You spanked me!" she said in a pained voice.

"And you'll be getting more than that, I assure you."

Immediate tears sprung in her eyes, but Jack took no heed. They had both been foolish and would be punished accordingly. Although he preferred to do it when she was sober, so she would remember and learn from it.

He looked over her head at Logan and saw that he was already leading Sapphire out of the barn. She was dragging her feet, but it made no difference. He looked back down at Sophia and saw her sway. Muttering an oath, he picked her up in his arms and, following Logan, strode out of the barn towards the main house. Sophia was too inebriated to fight him and her eyes fluttered closed with fatigue.

One thing was certain, these two defiant little madams would be getting a good roasting when they sobered up.

Chapter 10

SOPHIA AWOKE SLOWLY, opening one eye and then the other before quickly shutting them again when the bright sunlight filtering through the window hurt her eyes.

"Oooh!" she groaned, pulling the coverlet over her face.

Had they really drunk that much last night? Slowly, events from the previous night began to enter her mind and she quickly sprang upwards when she remembered how angry Jack and Logan had been.

God's bones. They were in trouble. She vaguely recalled Jack laying several heavy swats on her posterior and picking her up in his arms. She couldn't remember anything else after that. She glanced down at her attire and saw she only had on her shift. Had he undressed her? No. It would have been one of the maids, surely?

A tentative knock came on the door and Sophia said hesitantly, "Who is it?"

"Beatrice, miss."

It was Sapphire's maid. She quickly bid her to enter. The door opened inwards and Beatrice stepped inside, carrying a jug of hot water and a bowl. Placing it on the table, she smiled warmly. "This is for you to freshen up with, miss. And I have to give you this note."

She handed Sophia a note and went to leave, but Sophia stopped her by asking if she had undressed her. She was relieved to hear her say she had. Beatrice quickly left and Sophia ran a hand over her face, trying to wake herself up fully. Eugh. She really had to learn when to say no.

She looked down at the note on the bed. Who was it from? Intrigued, she unfolded the letter and scanned the contents, her eyes widening in alarm. God's bones! It was from Jack and it just read, *Don't leave the room. I will be arriving shortly.*

Her heart began to race. What did he mean by 'arriving shortly'? It could only mean one thing. He was going to punish her for last night. She vaguely remembered him saying that she was going to get more.

As much as her head thumped, she quickly rose from the bed, and splashing her face and arms with the warm water, she dried herself quickly with the towel and reached for her dress. But before she had a chance to put it on, there was a loud knock on the door. She could just tell from the assertive rap that it was Jack.

"Go away!" she called out, quickly running over to the door with the intention to turn the key but too late. Jack was already entering. His eyes fastened on hers. "Going somewhere?"

"What do you want?" she asked defiantly, edging backwards.

"You know why I'm here." He walked towards her, his eyes not leaving hers. Sophia gulped. How the devil was she going to get out of this? Her eyes darted to the door behind him and she quickly tried to make her escape, but Jack was on her in seconds. He caught her by the arm and brought her to a complete standstill. Her blonde hair swished around her shoulders as she came to an abrupt halt.

She half turned to look up at him and, seeing his intent, immediately tried to break free. "Let me go!" she shrieked, kicking out.

But Jack simply scooped her up in his arms and carried her writhing, protesting form over to the bed. He sat down and drew her straight over his lap.

Oh, no! He was definitely going to spank her. His hands were like iron. She struggled to stand back up, but his strong hands kept her in place.

She felt his hands on her ankles as he pulled her shift up and threw it over her back. God's bones, nothing was going to deter him.

"Jack, you don't have to do this. You spanked me last night. It was enough!" She tried to shift forward in the hope of wriggling off his lap and running for the door, but he simply wrapped one of his strong thighs over her legs and she was trapped.

"No, it wasn't nearly enough. You and Sapphire acted without a thought for the danger you were putting yourselves in."

His muscular arm wrapped around her waist and hugged her against his hips, allowing no escape. Sophia's stomach did somersaults and she tried once again to deter him. "But someone will hear us! It's not seemly."

"In this household, it's very common. No one will pay attention, believe me. But if you don't wish to share our interlude with anyone else, put your hand over your mouth if you must."

She realised that there was no way she could wriggle out of the spanking, and closing her eyes tight, she willed herself to be quiet.

She felt a sudden sting where his hand made contact with

her soft buttocks, then another and another. Soon, he was raining down swats, one cheek after the other, covering every spot until she was panting for release.

Her aim to remain quiet had long since gone.

"Ouch! Ooof!" Sophie whimpered, straining to get away. "Aow! That hurts! Ooh!"

She wailed miserably, tears forming in her eyes, but still, he didn't stop. The full impact of his hand made her body move with each stroke. His hands were huge, like the rest of him, and he made sure to cover every surface of her soft bottom with stinging smacks.

Finally, he paused. His hand rested against her hot bottom while he scolded her, his deep voice filling the bedroom, "You put yourself in needless danger last night. Getting inebriated and brandishing a sword at the same time! What were you thinking?"

Sophia realised he was waiting for an answer and managed to huff, "We both know how to use a sword. We're not stupid!"

His answer was to rain down several swats in quick succession that soon had her wailing for him to stop.

He paused again, leaving his hand settled on her sensitive skin. Sophia's backside felt as though it was on fire and she knew she wasn't going to be sitting comfortably at breakfast.

"So, my little spitfire, have you learned your lesson?"

Sophia nodded immediately. "Yes, most definitely. Absolutely."

"And you promise never to do it again?"

She nodded. At that precise moment, she would agree to anything.

Seeming satisfied, Jack rose from the bed and pulled her with him, placing her feet back down on the floor.

Her shift fell back down into place and she rubbed her

sore bottom gently through the thin material, refusing to meet Jack's eyes.

He, however, had other ideas. Placing his large hand on her jaw, he raised her face to look at him. His deep brown eyes stared down at her. In their depths, she could see that he cared a great deal for her.

His thumb caressed her cheek and her lips parted softly in response. His eyes fastened on them, a hungry look appearing on his face, and swooping down, his lips claimed hers. Sophia melted into his embrace. The fiery feeling in her bottom matched the fierce ardour she felt in her heart for this big, muscular man in front of her. His tongue fenced with hers, seeking to explore her succulent depths. Sophia felt herself grow wet with desire. If he decided to take her there and then, she would make no move to stop him.

Finally, Jack broke their kiss, breathing deeply and staring into her green eyes, now soft and dewy. "Now, when you're dressed, you'll come downstairs and join us for breakfast, and if you dare do anything so reckless again, I will have your bottom over my lap in an instant. Do I make myself clear?"

She nodded and her cheeks flushed with embarrassment. With one last look, he left the room, closing the door behind himself. Sophia raised a hand to her lips, feeling the softly bruised flesh where his lips had only recently plundered hers. Maybe she shouldn't love him, but she did. He was a disciplinarian, but he was also fair. Maybe Sapphire and she shouldn't have picked up their swords when drunk.

Sighing, she turned to get dressed, rubbing her painful bottom on the way over to the wardrobe. One thing was sure, she would damn well make sure Jack and Logan weren't in the vicinity if they ever got drunk again. She laughed softly to herself, her mischievous nature coming to the fore.

Fifteen minutes or so later, she made her way downstairs to the dining room. She stood outside the door and patted her hot cheeks to try to hide her embarrassment—she sincerely hoped no one had heard her being punished. But it was too late to worry about it now. Raising her chin slightly, she opened the door and entered the room.

She was relieved to see Sapphire was present, and pulling out the chair opposite her, she gingerly sat down, shooting her a quick smile. Sapphire responded likewise.

"Good morning, Sophia," Logan said.

"Good morning," Sophia replied, darting another glance at Sapphire. She was very quiet and Sophia wondered if she, too, had been punished, deciding that she must have. She had told her Logan spanked her and Jack himself had told her that it was common in the household.

"We're going into town this morning," Logan addressed the pair of them. "I trust you can behave until we return?"

"You know what'll happen if you don't," Jack added, his tone firm.

Both girls nodded quietly.

Scraping their chairs back, the brothers left for Bridport to meet up with Oliver and their father, Charles.

Sapphire waited for the door to close and then let out a massive sigh. "God's Bones! My backside is so sore!"

Sophia grimaced. "I gather Logan punished you?"

Sapphire nodded. "He lectured me about our reckless behaviour. On and on. Eugh." She looked at Sophia. "Jack spanked you, didn't he?"

Sophia nodded. "Did you… um… hear anything? I'm so embarrassed."

"Don't be. I'm used to it. Although, it's usually me who does the wailing. We're now comrades in arms, you and I." Despite her discomfort, she gave a low laugh. "We'll have to do some embroidery today to satisfy the men that we've learned our lesson well and will be good little girls."

Sophia frowned. "Really?"

Sapphire laughed wickedly. "No! Of course not!" She stood up and rubbed her bottom. "Although maybe we should stay away from the Bordeaux today." She grinned. "Now, eat some breakfast and we'll find something pleasurable to do that won't be boring but won't get us into trouble, either."

Much later, the women set off for a morning walk along the river. The day was beautiful and despite their tender backsides, they managed a nice leisurely walk along the embankment, taking in the local fauna and flora, both deciding that staying out of trouble was preferable to another spanking!

Two days later…

The time came to return to the ship in readiness for their departure and the return to America. Sophia bravely kept her tears at bay. She had enjoyed staying with Sapphire so much. She felt as though she was the sister she never had.

Bidding the family goodbye, including little Molly, she accepted Jack's hand as he assisted her into the waiting carriage. One of the grooms closed the carriage door and Jack leaned out the window.

"See you in a few months!" He banged on the carriage roof, and with a flick of the reins, the horses were set into motion and the carriage rolled out of the drive, the wheels trundling along the uneven surface.

Settling back in his seat, Jack looked at Sophia to see her eyes glistening with unshed tears. He immediately reached inside his jacket and brought out a clean linen handkerchief. Handing it to her, he said softly, "Dry your eyes, my love. I don't like seeing you upset."

She took the handkerchief and dabbed at the corner of

her eyes, trying not to sniffle. "What a lovely family. I'm going to miss them so much. I never thought I could grow so close to people so quickly. I think my father has ruined my view of life."

"I think you're correct, but you can change that. Your brother, despite our differences, seems a force of nature. I think he'll ensure you escape your father's clutches."

"I can only hope so."

The carriage rumbled along the bumpy roads until the port came into view. *Blythe Spirit* was looking as majestic as ever and Sophia felt a surge of excitement at going back to sea. Especially as she would be sharing Jack's quarters. She would make the most of the next few weeks, for it might be her last encounter with the handsome Jack Steel.

They reached the port and one of the grooms quickly jumped down and opened the door. Jack descended the steps first and then turned around to help Sophia down. Their luggage was unloaded and Sophia looked across to see Callum already running down the gangplank to assist them.

"Afternoon, Cap'n!" he said with a grin.

Jack clapped him on the shoulder. "I trust you had a good week on shore, Callum?"

"Aye, Cap'n. I even managed to cheer 'awkins up. 'E 'ad a face like a box o' frogs."

Sophia suppressed a grin. He was such a character. It was nice that he had managed to help Hawkins after what had happened with Natalie. Hopefully, being with his friends had taken his mind off love and all its tribulations. She knew that only too well.

Jack stepped up onto the gangplank carrying Sophia's luggage, and Callum followed with the rest. Sophia followed right behind, but halfway up, she remembered she had left her brooch on the carriage seat. She turned around quickly to see if the carriage was still there and was dismayed to see it was already halfway along the quay. Spinning back around, she suddenly felt her heel catch on the edge of the gang plank, and to her horror, she began to overbalance. Putting her hands forward, she tried to right herself but her angle was too great and she began to fall backwards.

She gasped with fright and flailed her arms, but it did nothing to help and she suddenly found herself free falling towards the water, several feet below. and then felt the breath knocked out of her body as she hit the water. The water closed over her, and she knew panic as she struggled back to the surface. It was cold, so cold. She struggled valiantly, but her heavy skirts seemed to be pulling her down, the fabric sucking up the water, becoming heavier and heavier.

No matter how hard she tried, her efforts seemed to be in vain and she began to sink deeper and deeper.

Jack turned around when Sophia shrieked and sprang into action. He was too far away to be able to grab her so without hesitation, he dove off the gangplank.

The water in port, although not crystal clear, was still thankfully clear enough to be able to see through. His eyes searched frantically for her.

He pushed himself deeper and deeper until he finally saw the flash of her blue dress. With a determined kick, he reached out with powerful arms and grabbed her around the waist, hauling her with him to the surface above.

They appeared with a rush, like corks bobbing in the water, both sucking in lungsful of life giving air. Sophia was coughing and spluttering, but she was breathing, Jack noted with much relief. Jack quickly pulled her to the side of the ship where John was already waiting on the rope ladder. The crew was leaning over the side, eyes wide, waiting to help if need be.

Jack handed Sophia to John. She was still in shock and had no strength to help herself up the ladder, but her small form was no problem for John. Scooping her up under one arm, he nimbly climbed the ladder up to the railings where several of the crew reached out and pulled her gently onto the deck.

Jack followed quickly behind, his lithe form jumping over the top railing to immediately take charge.

"Fetch Philippe. Tell him to wait outside my cabin."

"Aye, aye, Cap'n," Foster said, quickly disappearing below deck to fetch the ship's doctor.

Jack took Sophia in his arms and strode over to his quarters. Kicking the door open, he took her inside and laid her on the sofa. Sophia rolled onto her side, still coughing but seeming much calmer.

Going back to the door, Jack shut it tight before returning to Sophia's side. "I am going to undress you. You have to get out of these wet clothes."

"I can do it," she said weakly.

Jack shook his head. "You are in no fit state to be able to do anything."

He quickly divested her of the wet clothing, moving her gently as he went through the necessary motions. She made no further protest, letting him take charge. Reaching for a towel, he dried her as best he could, and then scooping her naked form up in his arms, he moved towards the bed and slid her beneath the warm coverlet, placing the towel beneath her head to soak up the excess water from her hair.

Making sure she was settled, he strode over to the door and allowed Philippe to enter.

"I think she's fine, but can you just look her over for my peace of mind?" Jack said.

"Aye, Captain."

Philippe checked Sophia over as Jack watched worriedly whilst divesting himself of his wet clothes and changing into dry ones. Her eyes were big in her face and her cheeks were as pale as snow. But after checking her pulse and feeling her forehead, Philippe declared her to be in good health, adding, "You're lucky, miss. Any longer, and you could have been a gonna."

"Thank you, Philippe," Jack said quickly. "I think she realises what danger she was in," he admonished him. Sometimes these men could be blunt to the point of rudeness. The last thing Sophia needed to hear was that she nearly died. She had had enough shock for one day. He ushered Philippe out of the cabin and closed the door behind him before returning to Sophia's side.

"I feel so foolish," she confessed in a small voice.

"Don't be. It's one of the hazards of being onboard a ship. But I'm certain you'll take more care in future."

"Absolutely. I never want to experience that again. I thought I was such a strong swimmer."

"The sea is sometimes unforgiving. Never forget." He took her hand in his. "I'm grateful that you weren't taken from me. I think you mean more to me that I realise."

She stared back at him, her eyes soft. He leaned down and kissed her softly. "Now, get some sleep. That's an order." He released her hand and stood up. "I'll return when we're underway."

He left her to rest and strode up onto the main deck. John was waiting for him. "How is she?"

"Very well, surprisingly."

"Thank the lord," he remarked before asking, "are you ready to depart as planned, or do you want to delay a bit?"

"Let's get going."

"Aye, Captain." John quickly began barking orders out to

the crew, his commanding voice spurring them into action. He was amazingly competent, highly knowledgeable in all areas. The men about him did his bidding unquestioningly and listened to him with open respect. They knew the consequences if they did not. The thought made Jack grin. He, too, found himself wary of the great man on certain occasions.

Jack took position on the quarterdeck of the ship as it sailed west out of Bridport Bay into the rolling blue-grey English Channel and then onward towards the vast expanse of the Atlantic Ocean.

Satisfied they were on course, and with the weather calm, he left control of the ship in John's capable hands and returned to his cabin to keep Sophia company. Having come so close to losing her, she was even more precious to him than before.

It had made him wonder if he would be able to let her go when they reached Jamestown. How would she feel about leaving? He had a lot to think about, and thankfully, there were several weeks before they arrived at their destination.

Chapter 11

AFTER HER TERRIFYING experience of falling into the sea, Sophia made certain to only go on deck when Jack was nearby. Added to which, he had warned her not to go out alone under threat of a harsh spanking if she dared defy him.

That had most definitely made her take notice.

So, she had taken to reading a lot and also studying Jack's maps. She found them fascinating. There were so many places to discover. So many places that she had never been. She decided that life onboard ship was far more exciting than being on land.

Jack said they would be stopping off for provisions again in Bordeaux. She just hoped she didn't encounter the odious Legrand. She chewed her bottom lip, wondering how Hawkins would feel. Would he try to contact Natalie again?

She tapped the polished wooden desk with her fingertips. One thing was certain, she wouldn't be offering to write any letters for him!

Shaking her head, she picked up the heavy glass magnifier and moved it onto the map laid out in front of her, her eyes focussing on the many different ports and beaches that they would sail past. It was fun, and she was beginning to learn so much about navigation. Jack had proved to be very attentive to her endless stream of questions and seemed genuinely impressed at how quick she was picking it up.

She loved spending time with him. He was not only gorgeous to look at but she found his deep voice soothing. Yes, it was time well spent.

When they reached Bordeaux in a few days' time, he had promised to take her to a restaurant. The thought brought a smile to her face, and for the next hour, she had a problem concentrating on anything else except the handsome captain.

That night, Jack was having a nightmare. Sophia was in the sea and no matter how hard he tried to swim to her, he just couldn't reach her. He could hear cannons firing from a nearby ship, the harsh noise insistent and never-ending.

Suddenly, he awoke, realising the pounding was coming from his cabin door. He blinked himself awake and rolling out of the bed, strode to the door and opened it.

Foster was standing there, his eyes wide. "Please, Cap'n. Grimes sent me. 'e asks ye to come on deck."

"I'll come," said Jack, quickly closing the door and donning his clothes. When Grimes called him like this, it meant it was urgent. If it wasn't, he knew he'd get an earful from Jack.

The faintest beginnings of dawn could be seen illuminating the mist as he strode onto the deck, and searching out Grimes, he quickly joined him. He was standing with his back to the wheel and appeared anxious.

"Listen, Cap'n!" he half-whispered as Jack appeared.

Jack kept quiet and listened hard. He heard the usual creaking noises as he would expect and the sound of the sea breaking beneath the bow, but then he heard voices. He frowned. They weren't coming from his own ship!

His eyes widened. "There's a ship close alongside!" he exclaimed.

"Aye, Cap'n," said Grimes, nodding his head in agreement. "If you listen 'ard, you can make out their words, and it ain't English."

Jack moved nearer to the rail and peered through the mist, but it was so thick, he couldn't see farther than two feet. Listening again, he heard someone shout and quickly recognised the language.

Walking back to Grimes, he confirmed the nationality. "It's French. Call all hands. Quietly now," said Jack.

His senses were on full alert. He had given the orders to send the men scurrying to their stations, but he had no idea how big the other ship was. Hidden by the thick fog, it could be any size. If it was bigger and decided to attack them, would they be able to defend themselves?

He consoled himself immediately. Perhaps she was carrying vast quantities of treasure—in which case, he would take her as a prize. He took out his spyglass and tried to peer through the thick fog, but it showed nothing.

"Jack, what's happening?" said a small voice beside him, and he nearly jumped out of his skin with surprise. It was Sophia.

"Be quiet!" he whispered furiously at her, and she gasped abruptly in astonishment. She was wearing her cloak and hood, wrapped up against the elements.

"I'm sorry. I didn't mean to—" she began.

"Silence!" whispered Jack and he added, "go back down below. Make no noise." He stared at her in the dim light and was satisfied to see she obeyed him immediately. The last thing he wanted was her exposed to danger. Not only that, but he had no wish for the other ship to know of their presence. If she thought his words harsh, it mattered not. In this situation, there was no time for niceties. Something that she would have to learn.

He heard a sharp voice through the fog and then a whistle being blown, followed by lots of noise and bustle. Then the ship's bell rang out.

His body tensed. Had they heard them?

John joined him. "What shall we do? Wait it out? Attack?"

"We need more light. We have no knowledge of her gun power." He raised his head and looked to his left. "The fog is beginning to clear. Tell the men to hold fast."

He stood, straining to peer through the mist across the dividing waters, and then suddenly, the mist began to clear, unveiling the vessel to their scrutiny.

"There she is! What a beauty!" exclaimed John, his voice full of excitement.

Less than a grappling hook length away, was a sleek French frigate standing parallel to them on their starboard side.

Without a moment to waste and with surprise on their side, Jack called out the order to attack. What ensued was a cacophony of noise and mayhem.

Jack's crew broke out the weapons and turned with relish to attack the other ship, who had been caught completely by surprise. The grappling hooks flew, and the French frigate found herself pinioned against Blythe Spirit's sleek hull.

Jack led the assault on the other ship, whilst John and the rest of the crew valiantly deterred anyone trying to board their own vessel. Grimes, his clay pipe still clenched between his teeth, leapt forward to engage a burly Frenchman who was attempting to gain the quarterdeck. The man soon found himself shoved overboard. "Take that, ye foreign bastard!" Grimes said with satisfaction, his eyes narrowing as he awaited the next marauder.

Sophia paced the cabin. She was as nervous as she could be. The sound of swords clashing, cannons and gunfire filled the air. It sounded truly terrifying.

What if Jack got hurt? What if he died?

She eyed the sword hanging on the wall for the umpteenth time, and then muttering an oath, she walked over and, standing on tiptoes, reached up and lifted it off its hooks.

Gripping it tightly in her hand, she walked to the door and listened. All hell was still going off. Her heart racing in her chest, she made the decision to go out onto the deck, and taking a deep breath, she exited the cabin.

No sooner had she set foot upon the deck, than she immediately had to side step a man falling backwards towards her. It was a near miss and she gasped with fright. Hawkins had just taken the man down and his eyes widened when he saw her standing in front of him. "Get back inside, miss. Ye can't be out 'ere!" he shouted above the ruckus.

She shook her head in the negative. She could fight and she wanted to help. Being stuck in the cabin and not knowing what was happening to Jack and the crew was driving her mad. Thinking of Jack, made her turn her head to find him. Seeing a clear passage between duelling men, she made a beeline for it and ran up the steps to the quarterdeck.

Her eyes darted to the other ship and she was relieved to see him alive. For a moment, she stood near the rail alone, something the French captain saw immediately. He quickly nodded to one of his seamen, and within seconds, the man swung swiftly across the gap between the two ships. Knocking the sword from her hands, he grasped her firmly about the waist and lifted her from the deck as the two of them swung back to the French ship.

Sophia turned on him with a shriek of fury, nails clawing, but her captor merely laughed. As she struggled with the man, she heard Grimes shouting across the divide to Jack. She looked across the deck to see Jack's face turn fierce with anger.

It made her more determined to break free and she kicked and struggled for all she was worth. She wasn't going to make this easy for him. He spat many French words at her that she didn't understand, but it did nothing in her quest to break free.

Suddenly, she heard a welcome voice right next to her. It was Jack. "Let her go, you bastard!" he demanded.

She turned her head and saw he was brandishing his sword straight at the seaman. She used the opportune moment to drop her body like a stone and, with a bit of wriggling, managed to slip through her captor's arms. She quickly stumbled away to safety, making herself as small as possible by crouching next to a large storage crate.

She watched Jack in fascination as he fought valiantly against the opposition. His strength and expertise was far superior to the Frenchman and it didn't take long before he had rendered the man unconscious.

Wasting no time, he swept Sophia up in his arms and, grabbing one of the ropes, swung them both back onto *Blythe Spirit*. Within moments, she found herself back in the cabin, the door locked and Jack having taken the key.

She knew by the look on his face that he was displeased with her for disobeying his command and leaving the cabin, but she would have to deal with that later. For now, all she could do was stay put and helplessly listen to the mayhem of battle.

———

Blythe Spirit's crew soon succeeded in overpowering the French ship and a great shout of triumph could be heard. The Frenchmen who were still able-bodied were tied up and kept under surveillance by two of Jack's crew, whilst the others were put to the task of unloading the ship's valuable goods onto Jack's own ship.

A little while later, when their cargo was plundered, Jack ordered his crew back to his ship. The grappling hooks were disengaged and, slowly, a border of water began to appear between the two ships.

Jack saluted the French captain, whose eyes narrowed in return.

"Reckon 'e'll want a bit o' revenge, Cap'n!" Grimes laughed, stoking his clay pipe.

"He might want it, Grimes, but he isn't going to get it." Jack laughed. Turning to John, he told him to take over command and he headed off to his cabin.

Sophia sat at Jack's desk sipping on a goblet of rum. She wanted something to not only calm her nerves, but give her courage, for as sure as eggs are eggs, Jack was going to punish her for going on deck.

The thought made her whole body shiver with a mixture of excitement and trepidation.

The door opened and he walked in. She stared at him silently, knowing by the look in his eyes that her punishment was imminent. She licked her suddenly dry lips and thought hard on how she could maybe wriggle out of a spanking. But nothing sprang to mind. She had already learned that when he threatened to do something, he usually carried it out. Oh, lord.

She shifted uncomfortably in the chair as Jack approached the desk.

"So what part of "stay in the cabin" didn't you understand?"

"I… um…"

"I very nearly lost you again. Are you so bored of my company that you seek to escape?"

"Of course not!"

He reached for her elbow and began to raise her out of the seat. "So, tell me, my disobedient madam, what you thought you were doing."

She tried to grip the edge of the table, but he shot her a look that silently said, 'don't even think about it', so she let go. He steered her over towards the couch and turned her around to face him, his face stern.

She looked up at him, her eyes wide.

Suddenly, his anger dissolved, and grasping her by the shoulders, he looked down into her face. "Why did you disobey me?" he demanded. "Don't you know how much I care about you?"

"It was because I care that I went in search of you. I was worried about you."

He tutted loudly. "I didn't know a woman could do this to a man—make him itch to spank her one minute and want to marry her the next!"

Sophia's eyes shot to his. "So, you want to marry me?"

"We'll discuss that later." He promptly sat down on the couch and quickly drew her down over his lap. She thought about fighting him but knew that it was futile. Her bottom was going to get a roasting, whether she wanted it or not.

She felt his hand on her ankle as he lifted the fabric of her dress and then he parted her bloomers, exposing her bottom. She closed her eyes, waiting for the first smack, but instead, his fingers cupped and kneaded her buttocks, sending a wave of emotion rushing through her. It felt heavenly, and for one moment, she thought she might avoid a spanking. But it wasn't to be.

Suddenly, she felt a stinging swat on her sit spot and she gasped.

He soon set up a steady tempo that had her wriggling and twisting to escape. But his grip on her was too tight and she had to endure his hard hand. She tried protecting herself by placing her hand in the way but quickly found it captured at the small of her back as he continued to mete out punishment on her backside.

Her bottom was heating up like a furnace and the pain was becoming unbearable.

"Please, Jack. Stop!"

"Uh-uh. You will learn to obey me. You're willful to the point of putting yourself in the way of harm and that, I will not tolerate."

His hand moved lower to her sit spots and smacked each cheek in turn several times, making her kick her legs, but his hand continued in exactly the same rhythm, loud slaps echoing around the cabin.

"Oow!" she cried lustily, wishing he would stop but knowing he intended her bottom to be as hot as a furnace before that should happen.

He smacked her several more times and then finally released his grip around her waist. She wasted no time in springing up from his lap and rubbing her poor, sore bottom better.

She pouted and sent him a sullen look, wondering why she was always getting in trouble with him. She had only been concerned for his welfare. There was no need to dish out such a punishment.

"Will you ever learn, I wonder, Sophia, or will you always have this stubborn streak that allows such willful behaviour?"

She raised her chin defiantly, refusing to answer him. He chuckled in response and stood up. "I'm going on deck. I suggest you take this time to think upon your actions and learn by them."

She watched him leave, and as the door closed behind him, she pulled a face behind his back. Trust her to fall in love with such a handsome devil.

She walked over to the bed and fell upon its soft surface, face down, and then shrieked into the coverlet with frustration. Would she ever learn to obey his command, or forever be thrown over his lap to receive a sound thrashing?

She closed her eyes and smiled to herself, already knowing the answer.

Bordeaux…

Sophia lay restless in her bed. She turned her head to look out the big, panelled windows, and through them, she could see the moon glowing brightly.

They would be arriving in the French port of Bordeaux within the hour, so Jack was already on deck overseeing their safe entry into port. She could hear the bustle and noise coming from the crew as they prepared for docking and the sounds were exciting to her. It would be fun to see around the port again. This time, she certainly wouldn't be writing any love letters.

She rolled over in bed and closed her eyes, trying to sleep, but they sprang open again. There was no way she could sleep. Slipping her legs from beneath the covers, she walked over to the chair, and taking her clothes off the back, she began to dress.

With her hair neatly plaited and her ablutions complete, she was ready to go up on deck. Quickly, she grabbed her cloak and left the cabin.

Jack stood on the foredeck, bellowing out orders to the crew. John was on the other side, doing the same. Under their experienced eyes, *Blythe Spirit* sailed into port slowly and methodically, her hull neatly cutting through the Gironde as she was directed to her moorings.

With the ropes secured, John joined Jack's side. "The holds are crammed to overflowing with spices from that French ship and we've a fortune in rare jewels. Reckon we should make a great deal of money from that lot."

Jack nodded in agreement. "Indeed, we shall." He looked at the horizon. "Sun will be up soon. I'll have breakfast and then we'll go into town. It'll be interesting to see how Legrand receives us."

John gave a low laugh. "Greedy bastard won't hesitate. He knows he'll make a rare profit out of this lot. Just you wait and see."

Jack turned around and descended the steps onto the quarter deck, to find Sophia standing at the rails, looking over at the quayside. He paused for a moment to drink in her beauty. The moon lit up her delicate features and her hair looked almost silver against the inky blackness from the river behind.

She had stolen his heart and he knew that when the time came to leave her in Jamestown, it was going to be very hard. But he had made a promise to her brother and he would abide by it.

She turned to look at him, and when she realised he was

staring at her, she sent him a soft smile. Oh, yes, she had definitely captured his heart, but did she feel the same way?

They still had a few weeks to go, so for now, he wouldn't worry about it too much. Walking over to join her, he asked if she was hungry, and then with a quick command to Smithy, he escorted her back to the cabin to wait for their breakfast.

Chapter 12

AFTER THEIR BREAKFAST, Jack scraped his chair back and stood up, informing Sophia that he was going to visit Legrand with John, to arrange the sale of their cargo.

"I think I shall go and visit that nice little boutique," Sophia said, her eyes sparkling. "She had some lovely dresses last time we were here."

She left the table and walked over to where she'd placed her cloak but stopped in her tracks when she heard Jack say, "You're not going anywhere."

"What do you mean I can't go?" Sophia exclaimed.

"Just that. You're not to step off this ship without me by your side. And that, my dear, is an order."

"But why not?" She almost stomped her foot in frustration but refrained at the last minute. It would only irk him and make him dig his heels in even more. In the short time she had known him, she knew that was a definite fact.

"All right, let's do some thinking here," Jack said, fixing her with a stare. "Should you go out and expose yourself to all sorts of dangers, which you seem to be adept at doing...

or should you stay here, where safety and peace are guaranteed?"

"This time, I shall stay out of trouble, I promise."

Jack raised an eyebrow, and then walking over to the cabin door, he opened it and bellowed up the steps, "*Callum!*"

Callum quickly appeared, and Jack, whilst looking at Sophia, said, "Fetch me some sturdy rope if you please."

Sophia rolled her eyes and, knowing his intention, exclaimed, "Fine! I won't go anywhere!"

Callum looked from one to the other, realising there was a battle of wills going on, and was mightily relieved when Jack told him to forget all about the rope and return to duty.

Sophia glared at Jack and spat, "I hate you!"

Jack simply laughed, showing his even, white teeth, and remarked, "Look at you. Saying you hate me, but I know that's not true. You love me, really."

Sophia's eyes narrowed and she looked around the cabin for something to throw at him, but Jack, seeing her intention, stepped forward and swept her into his arms. "Don't even think about it, my sweet." His eyes grew dark. "Unless, of course, you wish to receive another spanking?"

Sophia, disconcerted at having him so close, tried to shrug him off, but instead, he bent his head and claimed her lips in a fierce kiss. At first, she tried indifference, but it didn't work. His touch was electric, and soon, she was opening up to him, her hands clutching his broad shoulders, revelling in his expert touch. She knew she yielded too easily, but she couldn't help it.

Pulling away slightly, he looked into her eyes and she saw the evidence of his feelings, his desire for her obvious. He made no attempt to hide it. Her cheeks suffused with colour at his scrutiny and she lowered her lashes.

"Now, I will have your promise to remain on board whilst I'm gone," he demanded.

"Very well," she agreed. To be honest, she'd agree to anything at that precise moment—her emotions were haywire. But ever willful, she made her own demand. "But only if you promise to take me there this afternoon?" Her eyes shot to his, full of mischief.

"Hmm, you strike a hard bargain, you little devil, but, yes, I'll take you."

He released her and she grinned like a Cheshire cat. He turned her around and gave her a quick swat on her bottom and she yelped in surprise.

"What was that for?" she cried indignantly.

"Because I can." And on that note, he grabbed his tricorn off the table and with a little nod, he was gone.

Sophia pursed her lips. Arrogant devil. But then she thought of his kiss and her expression changed completely, a small smile breaking out on her face. Yes, he was a devil but wasn't that why she had fallen in love with him?

***

That afternoon, Jack took Sophia into town as promised. She had managed to behave herself all morning as she'd told him she would. The threat of being tied up or having another spanking was a good deterrent.

So after having lunch together in the cabin, he escorted her to the little boutique where she could buy her dresses. He handed her another little bag of silver coins for her purchases and was insistent that she didn't pay him back.

On the way back to the ship, she asked him if he'd managed to negotiate a good deal with Legrand for his cargo.

"Yes, amazingly, he was quite amiable today, although he seemed to take great delight in telling me that his daughter is going to get married to a local business man."

Sophia's face fell. "Oh, poor Hawkins. Will you tell him?"

Jack shook his head. "Not at the moment—maybe when we set sail. I do wonder how he'll take the news." He shrugged. "Legrand is coming to the ship later to pay for the rest of the goods. I think I'll tell Hawkins to keep a low profile, because if the two of them meet, it could mean war."

Sophia pulled a face, knowing that could very well happen. She decided to change the subject. "How long are we staying here?"

"A few days again, no longer. The weather's changing and I would rather reach Jamestown in clement weather. Storms at sea can be quite fearsome."

Sophia's eyes grew wide. "Oh, but your ship is strong, surely?"

"Indeed, she is. She has buff lines and a sleek hull, but an Atlantic storm can create chaos and even *Blythe* can find herself in troubled times." He shook his head. "It's not a welcome situation to find yourself in, believe me."

Sophia hadn't experienced a major storm at sea, and on hearing his description, she decided that she never wanted to. Not that she would have any choice, were they to encounter one during their voyage.

Leaving her in the cabin to sort through her purchases, Jack went to have a word with John about the upcoming visit with Legrand, his intention to tell him to keep Hawkins out of sight or at least warn him to hold his tongue. The last thing Jack needed was any more trouble.

In the early evening, Legrand arrived and was shown into Jack's cabin by Grimes. He directed a cursory glance at Sophia and then totally disregarded her. Sophia arched an eyebrow in response. Such a rude man. Why Jack did any business with him, was beyond her comprehension.

Well, two could play at that game. She looked back down at her book, pretending to read, but all the while listening to their every word.

Jack dealt with him very well, she had to say. It didn't take long at all. Legrand handed over the rest of the payment for the goods that had been delivered earlier, and after a quick goblet of wine, which he downed quickly, being the greedy pig that he was, he took his leave.

When they'd left, Sophia threw her book down and decided to follow them, half hoping Legrand would fall off the gangplank on the way off the ship or maybe trip over a rope and bloody his nose.

But unfortunately, that wasn't the case. They had stopped to talk to John and Callum, so Sophia remained a little out of view but close enough to overhear them. He had a big, booming voice so she certainly didn't have to strain.

She listened for a few minutes and realising it was just ship talk, she turned around with the intention to return to the cabin but then, out of the corner of her eye, she saw Hawkins appear from below deck.

Sophia's eyes widened. Oh, lord, this could create problems. She spun around just in time to see Legrand spot him. Perhaps that had been his intention all along.

Within seconds, Legrand was standing right in Hawkins' way. Hawkins looked very awkward and tried to bypass him, but Legrand stopped him by laying a hand on his arm.

"Going somewhere, boy?"

"Excuse me, sir. I 'ave work to do."

"Don't you want to know what's happened to my daughter?"

Hawkins' face flushed and his eyes darted to the ground. "It ain't my place to know, sir."

"That's right, it isn't, but I'll tell you anyway. She's engaged to a rich businessman now. Much better than the likes of you. Next time you want to declare yourself to a woman, choose one from your own filthy class."

Sophia gasped. How dare he humiliate Hawkins like that. She thought about stepping forward and giving him an ear full but knew that wouldn't go down well with Jack. She would just end up getting into unnecessary trouble yet again.

She stood silently fuming and then an idea came to mind. Her eyes lit up and she smiled wickedly before sidling off back to the cabin without anyone noticing. Once inside, she rushed over to the large wooden cabinet and, reaching inside, found what she was looking for—a slingshot. She had discovered it a few weeks back when she had been exploring everything in Jack's quarters. She hadn't used one for years. It was another weapon her brother had shown her how to use. All she needed now was a projectile. She opened a drawer and took several lead balls meant for Jack's musket. They would do. It might knock some sense into the horrible bastard.

Concealing the weapon in the folds of her skirt, she rejoined the crew. Legrand was still there, his pompous voice filling the air. Her lip curled at his tone. Arrogant pig.

She sought out Hawkins in the crowd. His face was beet red and her heart went out to him. What a callous individual Legrand was. Her hand tightened around the slingshot. Oh, yes, he had this coming all right.

Making sure no one was watching her, Sophia nonchalantly walked up the steps to the foredeck and settled herself between two storage crates, out of sight of everyone but right by the railings, so she could get a good shot at Legrand when he departed.

It wasn't long before Legrand made his exit. Sophia peered through the railings, watching him strut along the quayside. Now was her chance. Lifting the slingshot, she put one of the lead balls in the leather pouch and raised her hand, ready to launch her missile.

Suddenly, a hand clamped over hers. Shocked, she gave a little gasp and looked up to find Jack glaring down at her. Oh, lord!

"What do you think you're doing?" he demanded, ripping the slingshot from her hands. The small lead ball rolled onto the wooden deck and he quickly picked it up. Opening his hand, he looked down at it and then back to Sophia accusingly.

She flushed under his scrutiny, but her temper came to the fore. "He would have deserved it! I was only going to knock his hat off!"

Jack shook his head. "You never cease to amaze me. How can such a pretty little thing possess such a wicked nature?"

She stood up and placed her hands on her hips. "Well, you cannot deny that it wasn't warranted. He was awful to Hawkins just now. There was no need to be like that."

He tutted loudly. "I didn't know you had overheard, but if you'd stayed to listen, rather than taking off in a fit of temper, you'd have heard me rebuke Legrand for his lack of manners. As horrendous as he is, he did acknowledge that he shouldn't have provoked Hawkins so."

"Did he apologise?"

"No. I think an apology is far too debasing for someone like him. But at least he acknowledged his error. It's something."

"Odious man," Sophia huffed. "I still wish I'd done it, though. Just to see the look of surprise on his face, would have been priceless."

"Do you ever learn?" Jack asked her, tilting his head to one side and fixing her with a stern look.

"What do you mean?"

"That there are certain things you do not do."

"Fie, it's not for you to chastise me!" she exclaimed hotly, her eyes flashing fire.

Looking at her defiant expression, Jack's jaw clenched angrily. "It would seem, my little spitfire, that you need a reminder on how to behave." He pulled her protesting form to the steps leading down to the main deck.

She resisted him for a moment, but then when some of the crew began to notice something was amiss and started to stare, he noted she capitulated, allowing him to steer her towards his cabin.

Once inside, he wasted no time. Sitting down on the bed, he immediately laid Sophia over his lap, and throwing her skirts over her head, he began to smack her bottom. The loud slaps echoed around the cabin, mixed with small gasps of outrage from Sophia.

"You will learn to obey me. I can do this for as long as it takes, so heed me well."

Sophia kicked her legs in response and tried to wriggle forward, but he just gripped her tighter and smacked harder. She shrieked as his punishment continued to rain down.

He continued smacking her until his hand began to smart and her bottom radiated sufficient heat for him to know that she'd be sitting uncomfortably for a while. She was far too willful and had to learn to keep out of trouble.

Deciding she'd had enough, Jack threw her skirts back down and pulled her up, keeping a tight grip on her wrist. She rubbed her bottom through the material with her free hand, whilst looking at him sullenly.

"We set sail within a few hours. I trust you can behave on the journey back to Jamestown?"

Sophia lowered her lashes and her bottom lip pouted, but he noted she refrained from answering back.

So, releasing her wrist, he stood up and strode towards

the door. "Be good," he warned her, before leaving the cabin. He had a feeling she would obey, for today anyway. What tomorrow brought, who knew, but he would be quite happy to spank her pert little bottom every day if need be.

Smiling, he joined John by the wheel and prepared for departure.

The weather remained miraculously fair as *Blythe Spirit* sailed farther west. Even the treacherous Bay of Biscay remained relatively calm.

It wasn't until a few days had passed that a freak storm struck the ship—something Jack dreaded. The wind and waves were tremendous. The heavy rains soaked the decks and it took every member of the crew to keep the ship afloat.

Jack had ordered Sophia to remain in the cabin, but she had no intention of leaving. The movement of the ship rocking and rolling in the churning seas was terrifying and Sophia mainly lay on the bed trying to stop from falling off, hugging a pillow to her bosom for comfort.

Waves crashed against the hull, sounding like cannon fire, while the wind gave an answering roar. It seemed to last for hours and just when they thought themselves safe, the storm having died, the boom of a cannon brought them face to face with a pirate ship.

Jack and his seasoned crew soon had the upper hand and the unfortunate pirates quickly found their ship plundered, and they were sent off with a flea in their ear, wishing they had never attacked the larger vessel. Jack was exhausted but happy. His holds were now full of booty and he would have plenty to sell when he reached Jamestown.

When land finally came into view a week later, Sophia stood at the ship's rail and watched the undulating woodland scenery that sloped down to the riverbank pass by with mixed emotions. She dearly wanted to see her brother, but even though her relationship with Jack was fiery to say the least, she knew she would miss him.

One thing was absolutely clear to her, though—that her decision to leave home was the best move she had ever made.

Sunfire was already anchored off Archer's Hope and Jack moored his ship alongside. The time had come to set Sophia free, but it was with a heavy heart that he would do so.

Walking into his cabin, he found Sophia putting the last of her belongings into her carpet bag. She looked up when he entered and held his gaze. Neither of them spoke for a moment, both seeming to realise that this could be the end of their liaison.

Jack walked over to her, and reaching into his pocket, he drew out a small package and held it out to her. "You know that you are everything to me."

She blushed alluringly.

He continued, "But I want to give you room to make your own decision about a future together. I will leave you in your brother's safe hands and return here in two months. If you decide you want to stay with me, I will be a very happy man, but I will not pressure you into making such a life-changing decision at this moment in time. You need time on your own." He smiled softly and then added, "But know this. I will not give up this life. Not yet, anyway. But if you decide to marry me, I will buy us a house together wherever you like and we will have the best of both worlds."

He offered her the little wrapped parcel and she took it from his hands. Opening it, she found two ornate bracelets.

"Oh, they are so beautiful."

He took one and slipped it around her slim wrist, fastening the ties. He then put the other one on himself. Looking at her intensely, he explained, "When shared by two people, it will bring them together again someday. If you decide to remain with your brother, I will understand, but then I hope you meet someone who has a big heart, who can walk beside you, wish the same wishes, and love you whole-heartedly, for you deserve to be happy."

Tears sprung to her eyes and he gently wiped them away. "Do not cry, my love. Whatever you decide, I will stand by your decision."

His strong arms enfolded her in a warm embrace and she lay her head against his chest. He hoped she would know how much he loved her and return to him, but he wouldn't force her. She needed to come to that decision on her own.

Pulling away, he reached for her carpet bag and led her out of the cabin.

Chapter 13

ONBOARD *SUNFIRE,* Isaac led Sophia directly to the main cabin in the stern. She flung her cloak on a chair and sat down at the table, looking as miserable as could be.

Isaac frowned. "Was it awful, sis? I don't know how you stood it."

"No, it wasn't bad at all."

"Then why do you look so forlorn?" he asked, puzzled.

"I've fallen in love with Jack."

"What?" Isaac exclaimed, looking at her like she had suddenly grown two heads. "How can you have fallen in love with him? He held you against your will, for goodness' sake. Have you taken leave of your senses?"

Sophia scowled. "There's no need to be like that. It's how I feel."

Isaac threw himself down in a chair opposite her and put a hand to his brow. "I don't believe it." He leaned forward, peering at her. "Did he make you say it?"

"Of course, he didn't. Why is it so hard for you to accept?"

"Well, where to start?" he said sarcastically, "He somehow

managed to take you captive, tied me up, stole all our goods off our ship, which, I might add, was supposed to go towards us buying a house together!" He gave her an exasperated stare. "Did I miss anything?"

"You stole off him in the first place."

"Two wrongs don't make a right." He stood up again and paced the cabin. "Good lord. I wasn't expecting this."

"Well, I'm not going to lie to you. It's how I feel. He said he feels the same but will give me time to decide whether I want to make a life with him or stay with you." She fiddled with the bracelet on her wrist, taking comfort in the pretty keepsake Jack had given her.

Isaac sat back down and stared at her. "So, when do you have to give him your decision?"

"In a couple of months. He's returning to England, and when he sails back here, we will meet up and I will tell him."

Isaac raised an eyebrow. "I think I know what your decision is going to be. I can just tell by your face."

Sophia's lips twitched with mirth. Isaac could always tell her moods. "Fie, I might change my mind."

"No, you won't." His fingers thrummed on the table top. "Well, I guess that means I'll be buying a house of my own then."

"Yes. Talking of which, did you manage to gain any more money this time?"

"Yes! We happened upon a privateer and, being the kind souls that we are, relieved them of a nice stash of silks and spices," he said smugly and then added, "there would have been another but just as we approached her broadside, a damned rain squall hit, and we lost the bastard in a fog bank," he lamented, pulling a face.

"That was bad luck," Sophia commiserated.

"Tell me about it." He sighed. "Ah, well, might get the bugger next time." He slapped the table.

Sophia grinned at him and, reaching into her bag, pulled out a large bag of coins and placed it on the table between them. He eyed it quizzically.

"What's that?"

"It's from Jack. Half the share of *Sunfire's* booty. He felt it only fair to give us half."

Isaac raised an eyebrow. "That's a turn up for the books! The man does have a heart after all."

Sophia laughed. "Indeed, he does!"

"Well now, what do you want to do for the next two months until you see Jack again? Do you want to rent somewhere in Jamestown? Williamsburg?"

"Can't I stay on *Sunfire*?"

Isaac raised an eyebrow. "You know my thoughts on that."

"Yes, but I have just spent nigh on three months on Jack's ship. I have been through a storm. I've witnessed battles, I've fallen overboard…"

"Huh? You fell off the ship!" His face held a look of shock. "Well, that's decided then—a house in town it is!"

"But, Isaac, it was a mistake. I tripped and fell into the water and—"

"Don't bother. Nothing you can say will persuade me otherwise, so don't even try." He fixed her with a look. "After lunch, we'll take a trip into town and see what houses are available for rent."

Sophia pursed her lips, knowing that her brother could not be swayed and resigned herself to her fate.

A week later…

Sophia had settled into her new accommodations very well. They had found a small house on the outskirts of town, which was perfect, and although only temporary, Isaac had employed a maid, a cook and a gardener for her needs. They would also be able to keep an eye out for her safety whilst Isaac was absent.

He was due to come and see her tonight, so she had already informed the cook what meal should be served and had sent the maid off to town to buy some wine for the occasion.

Taking a seat on the front porch, she sipped on some iced tea and listened to the sounds of nature. The house was situated in a very tranquil area and out of sight of prying eyes. Something she had insisted upon. Her father wasn't too far from their location and the last thing she needed was him turning up on her doorstep. As far as everyone knew, her surname was Appleton. It was better to be cautious. The porch led down to a sizeable lawn and gardens, from which a long drive led down to a large, wrought iron gate. It was perfect.

Halfway through her drink, she saw a carriage pull up at the end of the drive and two people stepped out. She sat quietly, watching them as they began to approach her house, and something about them made her uneasy. As they drew nearer, she recognised her maid, Alice, being one of them, but the other one made her blood turn cold. It was her father!

He had a firm grip on Alice's arm and seemed to be pushing her along against her will.

God's bones! How had he found her?

She thought about running inside and locking the door, but Alice was clearly in distress and needed help. So she stood her ground, doing her utmost to look strong and unperturbed when, inside, she was feeling exactly the opposite.

She stood up and walked over to the balustrade to greet

them, her face as composed as she could make it, but her heart was beating ten to the dozen.

Her father stopped at the front steps and regarded her with dark, angry eyes. "Do you know how worried I have been or how long I have searched for you? Do you? You ungrateful little baggage."

He thrust Alice aside with no thought for her well-being and she fell to the ground.

"Father, have a care!" Sophia cried, rushing over to her. But before she had a chance to help her stand, her father's hand snaked around her wrist. "Let go of me!" she shrieked, trying to break free.

"Uh-uh. You're coming back home where you belong," he snarled, starting to pull her away from the house.

Sophia struggled, but it was no use. She looked to Alice, but she was clearly terrified and had her hands clasped together, her expression registering shock and fear. Sophia's father was a bully and he would certainly have frightened the poor maid. Maybe he'd even threatened her. She wouldn't put it past him.

She soon found herself thrust inside the carriage, and whether she liked it or not, she was on her way to Thorn Creek Plantation.

The next day dawned bright and cold. Sophia awoke and, for one moment, forgot entirely where she was. It wasn't until she rolled over in bed and opened her eyes, blinking slowly, that the full realisation of what had happened came to her with a rush.

Instantly, she sat up in bed, and seeing she was in her bedroom at the plantation, she placed her head in her hands and groaned, last night's events coming back to her.

She'd tried everything to reason with her father, but nothing had swayed him. All he did was rant about the distress she had put him through. It was all about him, as usual. No thought as to her well-being or why she'd done it in the first place and still insistent that she was a thief.

It turned out he had found her simply by luck, having overheard one of Isaac's crew talking about her at one of the local inns. He had simply sent his lackeys to do some snooping and had accosted Alice when she arrived in town.

Sophia had refused to dine with him last night, so he had dragged her to her bedroom and made sure that not only was the balcony door locked, but he had also locked her main door as well. There was no escape.

She sat for a few moments wondering what to do. She certainly wasn't going to stay here under his rule if that is what he was thinking. No way. But how to escape?

Slipping from beneath the covers, she quickly washed and dressed. Just when she was slipping her boots on, there came a tentative knock on the door. Sophia heard a woman's voice softly call out to her so she walked over.

"Yes?"

"Begging your pardon, miss, but Mr. Thorn wants to know if you will take breakfast with him."

Sophia thought about it for a moment and then decided to take the bull by the horns. She needed to assert her authority over him and let him know that she wouldn't put up with his actions. He had to release her and that was final.

"Tell him that I will."

Ten minutes later, her father unlocked the door and stepped inside. She stared at him silently, waiting for him to speak.

"I urge you to act cautiously. The servants have been told that you aren't to leave this house without my permission and they'll be severely punished if you dare step one foot outside.

So I suggest you think about that before making any hasty decisions."

"It would seem I have little choice."

"Good, then you understand me. Come, we'll have breakfast and you can tell me where you've been all this time."

Sophia followed him from the room. She would have liked to stay put, but the truth was, after having declined dinner last night, she was absolutely famished. So, reluctantly, she followed him down the stairs to the dining room.

During the meal, she told him only snippets of what had happened during her absence, refraining from mentioning Jack at all. The less he knew, the better.

"Do you still intend to send me to that school?" Sophia asked him, her eyes flashing with rebellion. "Because I shall tell you now, that I'm not going. I'm as resolute as I was when I ran away the first time and will have no hesitation in doing so again."

Her father shot her a look of derision, "It won't happen again, my dear, believe me."

He patted his mouth with a napkin and rang the bell. His manservant arrived and he told him to escort Sophia back to her bedroom, reminding her that said servant would be punished if she were to make a run for it.

With a heavy sigh, she did as she was bid.

Isaac was beside himself with rage. When he had arrived the previous night to dine with his sister, Alice had explained everything to him. At first, he had thought about going straight to his father and demanding Sophia's release, but knowing him of old, he knew he would never comply. He employed several men and an overseer on the plantation who wouldn't hesitate to turn a gun on Isaac were his father to order them to.

No, he had to think of some way of getting her out from under their father's nose without him knowing about it.

She had been in the rented house for not even a week, yet the evil bastard had already found her. What were the odds on that?

He glanced over at the ship next to him, *Blythe Spirit*. As luck would have it, she was still moored there, and as much as he distrusted Jack Steel, he also knew that he cared about Sophia as much as he did, so perhaps it was time to bury the hatchet and ask for his help.

The thought made him curl his lip. He just hoped he wouldn't be as arrogant as their last encounter.

Grabbing a rope, he swung over to the other deck and landed neatly in front of Grimes, who after stepping back in shock, quickly grappled him to the ground and manhandled him towards the captain's cabin, muttering under his breath, "Lord save me, 'e's come back fer more!"

Thorn Creek Plantation…

"Were you reading?"

Sophia looked at her father warily as he walked into her bedroom and answered, "Yes, as you can see." It was mid-afternoon and since breakfast, she had been ensconced in her bedroom.

"Then I will come straight to the point. I have arranged your marriage to Walter Longley's son, Tobias."

Sophia jumped up in alarm. "Marriage? What do you mean? I'm not ready to be married yet!"

"All you need to do is do as I say. He is known to be intelligent and capable. There's nothing for you to worry about."

"I'm not worried, but I refuse to marry him. You must revoke your decision. I only wish to marry someone I love. I certainly don't want to marry someone like him!" she protested.

He laughed, but his tone held no humour, "I forgot to add—you have no choice. The Longley's are a fine, upstanding family and will bring their wealth and prestige to join with ours."

Sophia stomped her foot. "I have no wish for my marriage to be part of some power game."

"I don't care for your wishes, daughter. You will do as I say, and there is an end to it."

"I will not!"

"He is arriving this afternoon, so I suggest you get used to the idea of marriage, but even if you don't, he's quite ready to accept you, even if you're unwilling."

On that note, he left the bedroom, locking the door firmly behind himself.

Sophia looked at the door and then slamming her book closed, she launched it at the door angrily. The ensuing thud echoed around the bedroom, giving her a smidgen of satisfaction.

How dare he arrange a marriage for her! She had only met Tobias once, and that was enough to know what a cruel, shallow man he was.

"Oh God!" she said aloud. "What am I going to do?"

Blythe Spirit…

Jack looked at Isaac in disbelief when Grimes, after a brief knock on the door, shoved him into his cabin. He was the last person he expected to see on his ship.

Isaac shot Grimes a look of exasperation and exclaimed,

"You can release me now. There's no need for this. I simply wish to talk to the captain."

"I ain't takin' no risks where yer concerned, laddie," Grimes hissed, his face fierce. He turned to Jack. "'E ain't got no weapons on 'im. Says 'e wants to talk to ye."

Jack looked at Isaac shrewdly. "Is that true?"

"Yes," Isaac confirmed and came straight to the point. "Sophia's been taken by our father."

Jack's eyes widened and he immediately stood up. "When? Good lord, how on earth did that happen?" Jack waved a hand at Grimes. "Release him."

Grimes shot a dark look at Isaac and said, "'arm the captain 'n I'll blow yer 'ead off. Understand?" He released him and stood back to the side of the cabin, keeping a steady gaze on the unwelcome guest.

Isaac pulled out a chair. "May I?"

Jack nodded briefly and then, irritated, said, "Why on earth has he taken her? I mean—how did it happen? I thought she'd remain safe with you." Jack slammed his hand on the table angrily. "Couldn't you keep your sister safe for even a week, for God's sake?"

"I'm renting a house for her on the outskirts of town. She's even using a pseudonym so how he came to find out, I have no idea. But he bloody well has and we have to do something about it!"

"Oh, so now you want my help?"

"Of course! If you care about her as much as Sophia thinks you do, then we must come up with a plan to rescue her." He stood up and went to leave. "But if you're a lying cove and have lied to my sister, then I shall do so alone."

"Sit down," Jack boomed. "Your temper is just like your sister's," he stated, shooting him a look of irritation. They were both hot-headed. He waited for Isaac to calm down and then, between them, they began to plan Sophia's rescue.

Thorn Creek Plantation...

Sophia eyed Tobias Longley from across the room. He was a tall, wiry man and possessed cruel eyes and thin lips which were usually curled downwards as though he had witnessed something distasteful. She had never liked him, yet here she was, expected to marry the scoundrel.

He was deep in conversation with his father and hers. No doubt planning the bloody wedding. Good lord, how had she got to this point? One minute, she had been happily dreaming of a future together with the handsome Jack Steel, and now she was supposed to marry someone she loathed.

She had to get out of this. But how? Her brother must have found out what had happened to her by now, but why hadn't he turned up to help? Where was he? She paused, her eyes widening. Maybe he had tried to help and her father had sent him packing. Oh, good Lord, what was she going to do?

She nibbled on a fingernail, trying to create a plan of escape. She could enlist the help of Loretta, but if her father found out she had been involved, then she would only get her into trouble. She loved her too much to put her through that.

No. She would have to find an opportunity to make a run for it. Deep in thought, she didn't notice Tobias approach until he was right next to her.

"Something troubles you," he stated. "If you wish to share, I'm all ears."

She looked up and gave him a tight-lipped smile. "Oh, it's a problem that is mine alone. But I thank you for your concern."

He leaned near to her ear and whispered, "I will have no secrets between us."

She could feel his breath on her ear and it made her

shudder. He oozed malice and all her senses made her want to run in the opposite direction, but she had no wish to cause a scene with others present. Taking a deep breath, she took a step backwards. "If you would excuse me, I have to go…"

"Go where? Are you scared of me, Sophia?" His eyes bored into hers. "I quite like the idea of you being fearful. I cannot lie, I find it quite exciting."

Sophia swallowed hard and stared at him. Fie, he was worse than she thought. What manner of a man was he?

"You take pleasure in my fear?" Sophia said, eyeing him warily.

"Indeed. Does it surprise you?" He didn't wait for her answer. "Not that it matters. Once we're married, you'll find that I have certain preferences and that I never take no for an answer." He reached out and, taking a strand of her hair, twirled it around his finger and, in doing so, pulled her nearer to his face. "So be as scared as you like, my sweet maiden. Whether you agree or not, you're to become my bride, and then I shall do as I like."

Sophia stared back at him and knew true fear. Staying at Thorn Creek Plantation was definitely not an option. She had to escape, for there was no way on earth she could submit to such an evil man.

Chapter 14

SOPHIA WAS in the midst of a nightmare when a sudden noise woke her up. She sat bolt upright in bed, breathing heavily, and placed a hand over her heart. It was racing. Raising her hand to her forehead, she could feel small beads of sweat on her brow. What a terrible dream. She had been running away from Tobias and he was just about to reach for her when, thankfully, that noise had awoken her.

She blinked sleepily and went to lie back down again but, suddenly, heard a commotion outside the front of the house.

Leaping out of bed, she went over to the balcony doors and, pulling aside the curtain, peered out. She could just about make out the front drive and trees lit up by the half-moon, but other than that, there didn't seem to be anything unusual.

Suddenly, a figure jumped onto her balcony and she fell back, covering her mouth to contain a small shriek of surprise. Her heart beating ten to the dozen, she moved forward again and, with fearful eyes, peered out.

Her fear dissipated as soon as she saw who it was. Jack! He had come to rescue her!

He placed a finger on his lips, signalling her to keep quiet, and then tried the door handle. It didn't budge, so he raised his hand and indicated that she should step back. She did so instantly. He aimed his shoulder at the door and on the second attempt, the wood splintered and the door sprang inwards. It didn't make as much noise as she would have thought.

"Sophia!" he whispered. "Grab your cloak. We don't have much time."

She took it from the chair where she'd thrown it and he placed it around her shoulders, drawing the clip together before placing a firm kiss on her lips. "We must hurry. Your brother and some of the crew are keeping watch. Can you climb down the ladder?"

Sophia nodded, her heart in her mouth with fear. If her father discovered them, all hell could break loose. She frowned, wondering how Isaac and Jack had managed to overcome their differences to join together in her rescue, but now was not the time for questions.

Walking outside, Jack led her to the railing, and lifting her up as though she weighed no more than a feather, he gently passed her over the top rail and maneuvered her until her feet were on the second rail down. She could see two men standing at the bottom holding the ladder securely, which gave her the confidence to climb down.

Nearing the bottom, one crew member took hold of her elbow and helped her with the last two steps. "Careful, miss."

She recognised Callum's voice and whispered a "thank you" to him. She looked at the other man and, in the moonlight, recognised Foster.

Jack quickly followed and the four of them ran towards the main gates. Suddenly, a shot rang out. Jack whirled around, thrusting Sophia behind him for safety. "Damnation!" he exclaimed.

She could see some figures running towards them and several others behind them. Then another shot was heard. Jack thrust Sophia towards Callum. "Get her out of here."

"Aye, Cap'n!" Callum grabbed Sophia's hand and began to run. Half of her wanted to stay and help, but she realised she would only be a hindrance. So, she did as Jack wanted and ran as fast as she could towards freedom, knowing that this might be her only chance.

Jack kept low to the ground and withdrew his own pistol. In the dim moonlight, he could make out Grimes, Isaac and Hawkins heading towards him. Right behind them, were several men from the plantation.

"Prime your weapon, Foster," Jack whispered. He waited until they were near and then fired a warning shot. It whizzed past one of the pursuing men's heads, causing him to curse loudly and then he returned fire.

"Aaargh!" Jack heard someone cry. The bullet had found a target. Incensed, Jack told Foster to do the same and then reloaded his own weapon and fired again. But still, the men came.

Grimes and Hawkins reached his side and it was then that Jack saw that it was Isaac who had taken the hit. His leg was bleeding and Grimes was supporting him. Isaac's face was tight with pain.

"Hawkins, Foster, get him to safety," Jack commanded. "Grimes, stay with me. We'll have these bastards."

"Aye, Cap'n. Bleeders will rue the day!"

Whilst Hawkins and Foster went towards the gate, supporting Isaac in between their broad shoulders, Jack and Grimes protected them as only they knew how—sheer determination and strength. When Jack was angry; nothing got in his way.

———

Sophia paced the cabin, worried beyond measure. What was happening? Were they all safe? What if any of them were harmed? She would go back and take revenge herself if that was the case. All this, because her father couldn't leave her in peace to live her own life.

A further ten minutes passed, and frustrated, she went out on deck to see if there was any sign of them returning.

Callum was standing on the railing, supporting himself on one of the ropes, his keen eyes scrutinizing the land for any sign of Captain Jack and the crew. He looked down when Sophia approached.

"What's taking them so long?" Sophia asked him.

"I don't know, miss. I can't see any sign of Simmons returning yet."

Simmons was on tender watch, ready to row Jack and the crew back to the ship. Sophia stared towards the shoreline and could just see a small light which was most probably Simmons' small lantern, but trying to make out anything else in the dark was nigh on impossible. She clasped her hands together nervously. John joined her.

"Don't worry, miss. Fighting's what we do best."

If only Sophia had his enthusiasm. Her father was a cold-hearted, mean bastard and would stop at nothing to get his own way. She just hoped no one came to harm.

A few moments later, Callum called out, "Tender's coming." He jumped down onto the deck and hurried towards the rope ladder along with several other men, ready to assist whoever was on the small boat. Sophia waited impatiently to one side.

As the tender drew closer and closer, Sophia could make out the occupants. Her eyes widened when she saw Isaac and she instantly knew he had been wounded by the look on his face. Hawkins and Foster were with him, but there was no sign of Jack. Her stomach sank. What if something had happened to him?

Nervously, she watched the men help her brother up the rope ladder. It wasn't easy, but between them, they hauled him upwards onto the deck. It was only then that Sophia could make out the dark stain on his leg. She gasped, "Isaac!"

"Sophia," he said weakly, "don't worry. It looks worse than it is."

Sophia eyed the blood running down his leg thinking that it certainly did look bad, but saying so would only make him feel worse than he already looked.

John took command. "Take him down to Philippe." Two of the men carried him towards the stairs and Sophia made to follow, but John placed a hand on her arm. "Rest here a while, miss. Let them get him cleaned up afore you see him."

"But I want to go!" she protested.

John shook his head. "No, miss. There are some things a woman shouldn't see."

Sophia chewed on her bottom lip. Although she wanted to be by her brother's side, maybe John was right. Instead, she focused on what Foster was telling another crew member, her ears picking up when he mentioned Jack.

She quickly joined them. "Foster, is the captain all right? Where is he?"

"Fending off the plantation overseer and guards. We're going back to help them now."

He quickly disappeared over the side along with three other crew members, expertly descending the rope ladder like agile monkeys. She watched Simmons row swiftly towards the shoreline and hoped with every fibre of her being that Jack was winning the battle.

Jack nestled down in the undergrowth and whispered to Grimes, "Looks like we've outrun them. We'll wait a few more minutes and then make our way to the shore."

Even though they had fired several shots, no one seemed to have taken a hit, and little by little, he and Grimes had managed to back away until they had taken cover in deep grass just outside the plantation boundary.

Quietly, they lay listening in the dark. Silence surrounded them, apart from the occasional bird call. Jack breathed a sigh of relief. It seemed the overseer had given up. He went to make a move and then Grimes stilled his arm.

"Listen! They've brought the dogs out!"

"Bastards!" Jack hissed. "We have to run for it!"

With no hesitation, Grimes jumped up with him and they ran like fury towards the marshlands, keeping as low as they could to the vegetation. But with the dogs on them, it was going to be hard to avoid another confrontation.

Jack gripped his pistol tightly. It was primed and ready to go; he was taking no chances.

He could hear the dogs getting nearer, their loud yelps and barks making a cacophony of noise in the dark of the night. But he wasted no time to stop and see how near they were. Time was of the essence. On and on, they ran, avoiding rocks, jumping over narrow streams until they eventually reached the beach. There was a mist creeping onto the land from the river and Jack had to narrow his eyes a bit to search out the tender.

His relief was palpable when he saw his crew stepping

off the little boat. He ran towards them, waving his hand and saying, "Shove off! Quickly now!"

"Aye, Cap'n!" Simmons immediately responded, shoving the boat back out. Jack and Grimes jumped in along with the other crew who already had their weapons primed and aimed at the dark marshland behind their captain.

By the time the dogs appeared on the beach with their masters, the tender was already halfway out and hidden in the bank of fog. Jack had never been more grateful for fog than right at this moment.

"Good lord, that was a close call!" he exclaimed, keeping his voice low, to avoid detection from their pursuers. Even through the fog, their voices could carry and a stray bullet might find one of them a target.

"Aye, Cap'n," agreed Grimes. "Reckon we'll all need a shot o' rum after that."

Jack gave a low laugh. "Why does it always come down to rum with you, Grimes?"

"Is there somethin' else then, sir?" Grimes shot him a wicked smile, making everyone laugh, the tense evening now, thankfully, a thing of the past.

As soon as Jack arrived back on his ship, and after reassuring Sophia he was unharmed, he set the crew to make preparations to haul the anchor. He knew Sophia's father would try to involve the law somehow to steal his daughter back, and he had no desire to wait around and find out.

John told him that Philippe was tending to Isaac, so leaving John to oversee the crew in his usual gruff manner, Jack descended below decks to see how he fared.

Isaac's leg was bandaged and he was lying on the table,

beads of perspiration on his brow. He smiled wryly when he saw Jack.

"How's the wound?" Jack asked him.

"It hurts."

Philippe walked over, wiping his hands on a cloth. "It was a surface wound, luckily for him. It didn't hit any bones. It's quite clean so should heal quickly seeing as he's so young 'n healthy." He patted Isaac on the shoulder. "Reckon you should stay here a while to rest. The least movement, the better."

Isaac shook his head. "I've got to get back to my own ship. Now I know Sophia's safe, I can leave."

"I don't recommend it, lad," Philippe said, shaking his head. "If that wound gets infected, you could lose your leg."

"Well, that's settled then. Welcome to *Blythe Spirit*, Isaac!" Jack grinned.

"But—"

"No buts. I'll send a message to your ship to follow us out into the Atlantic. They can keep close by until you're recovered. I trust you have enough provisions onboard?"

"Yes, we do, but surely, I can go back on my own ship." He looked at Philippe. "How long will I have to stay here?"

"All depends. Could be a week or two, could be longer for it to heal. Everyone's different. But if you haven't got a fever within the next three days, then I'd say you're safe to go. But you'll still have to rest." He raised an eyebrow, daring Isaac to defy him.

Isaac sighed but nodded resignedly. "Very well. Three days is acceptable, I guess."

Jack chuckled, knowing how frustrated he must feel, but sometimes in life you had to take the good with the bad. He shot him a look of commiseration and said, "Think upon it as a well-earned rest. I know for one thing that your sister will be delighted to have you on board."

Isaac's face softened for a moment and he nodded. "It will be good to spend some time with her."

Jack left him in the sick bay, under Philippe's watchful eye, and headed back to his cabin.

Sophia sat at the window seat staring forlornly out into the fog. It matched her mood to perfection. Damp and grey.

Everything had seemed to be so settled and then her father had come in and ruined her life once again. Why couldn't he just leave her alone? Did he truly think that she would just meekly submit to his will and marry such an evil man as Tobias?

Her lips tightened with anger and her hands balled into fists. One thing she was in no doubt about was she could never go back there again. Ever.

But more to the point, what was she going to do now? Her poor brother was wounded. How badly, she knew not.

She sighed and closed her eyes. All this was giving her a headache.

Suddenly, the door opened and Jack appeared. She jumped up and ran over to him. "How's Isaac? Is the wound bad? Will he recover?"

Jack placed his hands on her upper arms and immediately reassured her. "He's fine. Philippe has dressed his wound which is only superficial. So you've no need to worry."

"Oh, thank goodness!" Sophia breathed. "And you? Are you unharmed?"

Jack smiled. "Are you worried about me?"

"Of course, I am!" She lowered her lashes a little. "Thank you for rescuing me."

He placed his hand on her chin and tilted her face to his.

"As soon as your brother told me what had happened, we devised a plan together. Your father didn't hurt you, did he?"

Sophia shook her head. "No, but he did intend to marry me off."

Jack's eyes darkened with anger. "To whom?"

"One of his business acquaintances, Tobias Longley. A horrible, spiteful man. Neither of them cared that I wouldn't comply and told me it would go ahead anyway! How dare they!" she exclaimed furiously.

Jack drew her against him, placing his arms around her back and waist for comfort. "It's over now. It was an ordeal you should never have experienced, but take solace in the fact that you'll never have to see them again."

She felt her anger dissipate as his words sank in and she realised she was safe. She also understood that this was exactly where she wanted to be. She had no reason to wait for the two months he had insisted upon. This was the only man she wished to marry.

She pulled away a bit so she could look up into his face. He stared back at her, and before she could speak, he said, "Did I tell you that I'm in love with a beautiful woman?"

"Y-you are?"

Jack nodded and continued, "She's standing right in front of me."

"Oh, Jack, do you truly love me?"

He smiled. "More than life itself. I'm not willing to wait two days, let alone two months, to wait for your answer. So tell me now, will you be mine?"

Sophia answered without hesitation, "Yes!"

He lowered his head and claimed her soft lips in a loving kiss. All Sophia's worries melted away and she knew that she was where she was meant to be.

He pulled away a little and said, "Now, I'll treat you as

the most precious woman in the world. No one will ever harm you again. They have to come through me first!"

He dipped his head again to kiss her more deeply, his tongue fencing with hers, and that soon had them both gasping with desire. Finally, he broke away. "Come and see your brother before I give in to temptation."

Sophia smiled wickedly and, reaching up, nipped his lower lip gently. "Maybe I want you to give in to it."

He growled and nuzzled her neck. "You're playing with fire, my love." He pulled away and, grabbing her hand, pulled her towards the door. She thought about playing some more, but her desire to see her brother overcame it and, obediently, she complied.

Isaac's face lit up when he saw her. "Sophia!"

He was lying on a small bed with his upper body raised by several pillows. She ran to him and embraced him, taking care to stay away from his leg wound. She pulled away and inspected the bandage.

"I'm so sorry, Isaac."

"Don't be sorry, Sophia. We both know our father is the instigator in all this. The man's unhinged. I still cannot believe that he found you."

"Neither can I. He has his spies everywhere, it seems. I do hope Alice is all right. He pushed her to the ground without a thought for her well-being!" Her eyes narrowed, remembering his odious behaviour.

"She's fine, more angry than harmed. She was the one who told me what happened."

"Oh, thank goodness." Sophia breathed a sigh of relief and then she asked him, "Do you remember Tobias Longley?"

Isaac nodded. "What of him?"

"Father was arranging my marriage to him, even though I was against it."

Isaac's jaw fell open. "Marriage! Good lord, what was he thinking? Thank goodness we were able to rescue you."

"I'm never going back. In fact, I intend never to come back to Jamestown at all. Jack and I are going to be married."

Isaac's eyes widened. "Well, that was decided more quickly than intended."

"Our father thought to intervene in my life, and he certainly did, although not in the way he intended!"

Isaac reached for her hand, "As long as you're happy, sis, then I stand by your decision."

She kissed him on the cheek and smiled. "Just make certain you don't attack his ship again."

He chuckled. "No, that I can promise." He grimaced a little and looked down at his leg. "Got to heal this before I do anything. I'm staying on board for a few days and then, all being well, I can return to *Sunfire.*"

"Oh, good. We can spend some time together. Are you hungry? I'll ask Smithy to make one of his delicious stews." With a quick kiss on his cheek, she quickly went off on her quest, leaving Isaac shaking his head. She was a little whirlwind and it was clear to see that she was happy. That was all he could ask.

That night, as they prepared for bed, Jack gathered her into his arms and kissed her tenderly. "I will treasure you always, my sweet Sophia." Softly, his lips pressed upon hers and then he murmured, "I want to make love to you."

"I want you to as well, but we are not wed, Jack. Should we not wait?" she whispered, already feeling herself succumbing to his masculinity and fearing she wouldn't be able to resist.

"You're going to be my wife," he replied firmly. "Why should we wait?"

With expert fingers, he unlaced her chemise, pushed it from her shoulders, and caressed her pert, rounded breasts. Sophia arched her neck when his lips covered her nipples, teasing them into rosy, red perfection.

His kisses trailed a line up to her throat, her jaw and then to her cherry ripe lips, which he claimed once again. She was lost to his touch and there was no going back. She felt his hands at her waist and he drew her shift off completely. It fell to the floor, quickly followed by her bloomers until she was completely naked.

He lay her down on the bed and began to kiss her body with soft, sensuous kisses. Sophia revelled in his touch, feeling a longing to experience true love-making with this strong man who would soon be her husband.

She writhed beneath him as he slid his hot, wet tongue between the valley separating her breasts. Then he moved lower down her belly and then lower still, until he reached the secret place between her thighs.

"Oh!" Sophia moaned, half wanting to stop him but at the same time, how could she? The feeling was exquisite and her body craved every touch.

She was afire with longing and her thighs parted, eager to experience his intimate exploration. His hot tongue ran over her little sensitive pearl, igniting her senses until she thought she could take no more, and then, suddenly, her whole body tensed as she reached her pinnacle. The exquisite sensations rippled through her slender body. It was wonderful!

Jack moved up her body and his mouth came down upon hers, cutting off her cries of joy. He slipped his hands beneath her hips and carefully positioned himself, moving forward, pushing himself gently into her body. He didn't want to hurt her, so he took things as slowly as his aching cock would allow.

He felt her tense at his entry and knew she was a bit frightened. "I'll try not to hurt you, my love."

Her fingers dug into his broad shoulders and she clung onto him, but she did not deny him. He knew she was as aroused as he, so, gently, he pushed forward, burying his manhood in her welcoming warmth.

She gave a small gasp but did not cry out. He stilled himself for a moment, to allow her body to get used to his size, and then unable to hold off any longer, he began to thrust and withdraw until Sophia was gasping with obvious, open pleasure.

Her small cries of delight were music to his ears.

His hips pumped against her, getting more frantic as he neared his pinnacle, but he would wait until she attained her crisis before he gave in to his own desires. He captured her lips once more, tasting her sweet breath and revelling in her response to his love-making. She was beautiful and now, finally, she was his.

Her fingers tightened on his skin and he felt her body vibrate beneath him as she reached her crest. With a few more thrusts, he allowed himself the pleasure of his own release and collapsed over her, mindful of his weight.

Sophia closed her eyes and smiled softly, loving the languorous feeling that making love had elicited. There had been a tiny bit of pain at first, but it had disappeared as quickly as it had come and she knew that Jack had done his best to make her first time special.

He moved off her and, drawing the coverlet over them, pulled her slender body against his. She lay her hand on his chest and snuggled into his arms.

"Did I hurt you?" Jack asked her with concern.

"Only a little bit, but afterwards, it was wonderful." She smiled wickedly. "I think we should do it often."

With a contented laugh, he tightened his embrace, kissing the top of her head. "I think that's one of the best ideas you've ever had."

And that was how Sophia had come to be on board *Blythe Spirit*. And why she was currently the owner of a very sore bottom, a predicament she often found herself in, and staring at the man she loved with all her heart.

As much as his discipline hurt, she wouldn't have it any other way. Jack Steel had come into her life when she needed him most, and for that, she would be forever grateful.

Maryse Dawson

Maryse Dawson was born in England but now lives in western France with her family. When she's not writing, she spends her time visiting the beaches and surrounding countryside.

She has always enjoyed reading romances and loves history, so began writing a few years ago to include domestic discipline in her stories.

You can find Maryse on Facebook at:
https://www.facebook.com/maryse.dawson.5

Don't miss these exciting titles by Maryse Dawson and Blushing Books:

Pirates of Steele
Sapphire and Steel
A Pirate's Prize

Loving Lydia
Lost Love
A Kingdom Divided
Dark Secrets, An Anthology
A Knight to Remember
The General's Discipline
Mischief by Moonlight
Summer Scorchers
Royal Reward

Victorian Vixen
Protecting Aleida
A Pirate's Temptress

Knights of Normandy series
Renaud, Book One
Arthur, Book Two
Gerard, Book Three

A Pirate's Treasure Series
A Pirate's Treasure
A Pirate's Stowaway
The Captain's Lady

The Beauty Series
Innocent Beauty, Book One
Seductive Beauty, Book Two

Moorland Maidens Series
Rhona, Book One
Heather, Book Two
Alana, Book Three

Anthologies
Feisty Fables
Brat Tales Book One
Brat Tales Book Two
Beloved Brats
Devious Maidens
Romantic Tales
Lords & Ladies
Historical Heroes

Blushing Books

Blushing Books is one of the oldest eBook publishers on the web. We've been running websites that publish spanking and BDSM related romance and erotica since 1999, and we have been selling eBooks since 2003. We hope you'll check out our hundreds of offerings at http://www.blushingbooks.com.

Blushing Books Newsletter

Please join the Blushing Books newsletter
to receive updates & special promotional offers.
You can also join by using your mobile phone:
Just text BLUSHING to 22828.